The two of them alone on Cape Cod?

That would be lunacy, Lacey thought, stunned by Kevin's suggestion.

Cape Cod was where they'd made love for the first time. Cape Cod was where he'd proposed to her. Cape Cod was where Jason had been conceived. Cape Cod was chock-full of memories. She had no intention of submitting herself to that kind of torture.

"No," she said adamantly. "Absolutely not."

"It would be so good for us, Lacey...."

The Cape had been their refuge, a place for quiet talks, long walks...and slow, sensuous sex. Of all the suggestions he might have made, this was the most wickedly clever. The memories they shared there were among their most powerfully seductive.

She met his gaze—and saw that he knew exactly what he was asking of her....

Dear Reader,

Welcome to Silhouette **Special Edition** . . . welcome to romance. Each month, Silhouette **Special Edition** publishes six novels with you in mind—stories of love and life, tales that you can identify with—romance with that little "something special" added in.

This month, we're pleased to present the conclusion of Nora Roberts's enchanting new series, THE DONOVAN LEGACY. *Charmed* is the story of Boone Sawyer and Anastasia Donovan—and their magical, charmed love. Don't miss this wonderful tale!

Sherryl Woods's warm, tender series—VOWS—will light up this Thanksgiving month. *Honor*—Kevin and Lacey Halloran's story—will be followed next month by *Cherish*. The vows that three generations of Halloran men live by create timeless tales that you'll want to keep forever!

Rounding out the November lineup are books from other favorite writers: Arlene James, Celeste Hamilton, Victoria Pade and Kim Cates. This is truly a feast for romance readers this month!

I hope that you enjoy this book and all the stories to come. Happy Thanksgiving Day—and all of us at Silhouette Books wish you the most wonderful holiday season ever!

Sincerely,

Tara Gavin
Senior Editor
Silhouette Books

SHERRYL WOODS

HONOR

Silhouette®

SPECIAL EDITION®

Published by Silhouette Books New York

America's Publisher of Contemporary Romance

SILHOUETTE BOOKS
300 East 42nd St., New York, N.Y. 10017

HONOR

ISBN: 0-373-09775-1

First Silhouette Books printing November 1992

Printed in the U.S.A.

SHERRYL WOODS

lives by the ocean, which, she says, provides daily inspiration for the romance in her soul. She further explains that her years as a television critic taught her about steamy plots and humor; her years as a travel editor took her to exotic locations; and her years as a crummy weekend tennis player taught her to stick with what she enjoyed most—writing. "What better way is there," Sherryl asks, "to combine all that experience than by creating romantic stories?"

The Halloran family requests
the honour of your presence
as Jason Halloran & Dana Roberts Halloran
and Kevin Halloran & Lacey Grainger Halloran
reaffirm their love
and renew their matrimonial vows
and
as Brandon Halloran & Elizabeth Forsythe Newton
enter a new life together.
Please share in their joy
at ten o'clock in the morning
on the twenty-first of June
at Whitehall Episcopal Church,
Boston, Massachusetts.

Prologue

Even at forty-eight Lacey Grainger Halloran was still one hell of a woman, her husband thought with pride and a sense of wonder as he watched her begin the long walk down the carpeted aisle of Whitehall Episcopal Church. She had never looked more stunning or more confident.

More than twenty-five years of marriage, Kevin Halloran thought. So many troubled times, shared and apart. Yet it felt as if they were starting out fresh, as if this were the very first ceremony in which they would make a commitment for life.

Last time, like so many of their friends in the mid-sixties, Kevin and Lacey had skipped the traditional prayer book, church wedding in favor of a hastily arranged outdoor ceremony atop a country hill alight with the colors of spring. Kevin's family, firmly entrenched in tradition, had been appalled. Throughout the brief service, with its unorthodox but heartfelt vows, their faces had radiated disapproval. But at least they had come.

Though Lacey had sworn it didn't matter, Kevin had known that deep down she had feared his family would stay away, publicly writing off the match as a bad one. It had nearly broken his heart to see the relief and hope in her eyes when she'd seen his parents join the small gathering on that sunny hillside.

Today's ceremony, a renewal of their vows, was every bit as significant as that first wedding day. His father and his son stood next to him, each nervously awaiting their own brides.

Kevin had been astonished to discover that long ago his father had been deeply in love with a woman whose name Kevin had never even heard mentioned. Now, just a few years after his own mother's death, that woman—Elizabeth Forsythe Newton—had reappeared in his father's life. Today they would be wed as his father had longed for them to be all those years ago.

With a sense of amazement, Kevin watched the transformation of his father's stern face as his bride began the walk down the aisle. After two long years of sorrow and loneliness, Brandon Halloran looked downright invigorated by life. His damn-the-world, full-steam-ahead energy was back, and everyone was having difficulty keeping up with him.

Something warm stole through Kevin as he realized that it was possible for love to endure through so many years of separation.

Filled anew with a surprising sense of hope, Kevin glanced at his son and caught the expression of open adoration in Jason's eyes as he waited for his wife to join him to renew their own vows. Within weeks Jason and Dana would be blessed with a child of their own—a boy if Kevin knew anything at all about the Halloran genes. The cycle would begin again.

All in all, it was quite a day for the Hallorans, Kevin thought as he took his wife's slender hand in his. Lacey was trembling, he realized with a faint sense of amazement. He gazed into her eyes, blue and bright with unshed tears, and realized anew how very deeply he cared for her and how devastated and lost he would have been had they not found their way back to each other.

Squeezing Lacey's hand for reassurance, Kevin began to speak. With his voice choked with emotion, he tried to find the words to tell her exactly what she meant to him, to express the strength he found in their marriage, had always found in her love. They were words he hadn't said nearly enough through the years, words he had almost lost the chance to say at all.

"Lacey, from the day I first saw you back in the fifth grade, there has been no one like you in my life. You have been my friend, my confidante, my lover and my wife. I am a better man for knowing you and loving you. I beg your forgiveness for the times I have forgotten that, for the times when I have lost sight of all that truly matters."

The memory of how hard his gentle Lacey had fought to save their relationship brought a smile to his lips. "I can't begin to find the words to tell you how much I admire the courage it took to shake up our marriage in the hope that we would find something even better. From now on I promise you days that will only get better with each passing year."

As a tear spilled down her cheek, he gently brushed it away, his own fingers trembling. Then he said in a voice that finally held steady, "I, Kevin, take thee, Lacey, a woman who has stood by me through hard times and good, who has provided love and understanding, I take thee again to be my wedded wife. For the blessing of your undying love, I thank God. For the joy of our family, I thank you. And I promise to honor you and all that you have meant to me all the rest of my days."

As the solemn vows echoed in the old Boston church, his thoughts drifted back over those dark and lonely days when his own stupidity had almost cost him the most important thing in his life.

Chapter One

"Dad, you're killing yourself."

Kevin Halloran tore his gaze away from the bleak Halloran Industries financial report he'd been working on for the past twelve hours and met his son's troubled eyes. "Jason, I am not having this discussion. Go home. It's after eight. Dana will be wondering where you are."

To Kevin's deep regret, his son defiantly removed his jacket and loosened his tie with the obvious intention of settling in for a lengthy chat. Kevin had a hunch they were headed over the same familiar turf. The sorry state of his marriage had been the primary topic of conversation for two weeks now. His son and his father couldn't seem to stop their meddling no matter how rudely he tried to cut them off.

Kevin reached for a cigarette, then caught Jason's disapproving frown as his son eyed the mound of butts already overflowing the ashtray. Kevin drew his hand back and settled for another sip of cold, bitter coffee. The acid pitched in his stomach.

"Dana knows exactly where I am," Jason said, complacently ignoring his father's dismissal. "She sent me. We're both worried about you, Dad. You look like hell. You're smoking too much. You're living on caffeine. I doubt you're getting enough sleep. Face it, you haven't been yourself since Mother moved out of the house."

The cold knot that formed in Kevin's stomach every time he thought about home and Lacey came back with a savagery that stunned him.

"I don't want to talk about your mother," he countered bluntly and reached for the cigarette, after all. When it was lit and he'd drawn the smoke deep into his lungs, he deliberately forced his attention back to the stack of work on his desk.

If he buried himself in reports and figures, maybe, just maybe, Jason would give up and go away. More importantly, maybe he could forget the emptiness Lacey's leaving had created inside him, the echoing silence that greeted him each night when he returned home.

In theory it should have worked, but Kevin had discovered that theories and paperwork didn't mean a damn thing in the middle of another god-awful, lonely, silent night. That didn't mean he was willing to talk, not to Jason. Lacey had been the only person in his life to whom he could open up. She had had the most amazing knack for listening without making judgments.

Jason obviously thought that his cool, analytical approach would help, but in Kevin's experience, talking about emotions never accomplished a thing. To his way of thinking, airing problems only exposed a man's weaknesses right at a time when he needed every shred of pride he had left.

Besides that, dissecting things a man couldn't change only made the hurt worse, Kevin thought, still careful to avoid Jason's increasingly impatient gaze. There were even times, in the dark, lonely hours of the night, when the pain became a blind rage, when he wanted to strike out, to break things. The only thing stopping him was the certain knowledge that he had only himself to blame for the way things were between him and Lacey. She'd made that clear enough before she'd gone.

"*I* want to talk," Jason said, still on the same relentless track despite his father's obvious unwillingness to open up.

His tone was deceptively mild. Kevin recognized the stubborn streak his son had inherited from a long line of mule-headed Halloran men. Even as Kevin glanced up, Jason was settling more comfortably into the chair opposite him, his jaw squared, his expression determined. He took Kevin's just-lit cigarette and deliberately ground it out, his hard look daring his father to challenge the action.

"Not once in all these months have you explained why Mother moved out," his son said.

"That's between your mother and me," Kevin responded stiffly, unwilling—unable—to say more. Then, because he needed desperately to know despite everything, he asked, "What has she told you?"

"About as much as you have," Jason admitted with obvious disgust at the continued parental secrecy. "Did you two make some sort of pact of silence, the way you always did when I was a kid?"

"We never did any such thing."

"Perhaps it wasn't a formal contract, drawn up by the Halloran legal staff, but it was a pact nonetheless. You never wanted me to guess that the two of you were quarreling. Instead, the house got quiet as a tomb for weeks on end." He shook his head. "It was awful."

Unable to bear his son's distraught expression, Kevin stood up, walked to the window and stared out at the Boston skyline in the distance. Lights were just now blinking on. Was one of them Lacey's? he wondered. What was she doing in that ridiculously cramped apartment of hers? How could she hope to find happiness there, when he'd given her everything a woman could possibly want and it hadn't been enough?

He sighed and turned back, just in time to hear Jason say, "When Dana's mad at me, she puts all her cards on the table, usually at the top of her lungs. There's not a chance in hell I won't know exactly what's on her mind. With the two of you, though, I don't know." He shrugged helplessly. "I think I'd have liked it better if you'd broken the china."

"And risked your grandfather's wrath?" Kevin retorted with a faint smile. "That china came over from England more than a century ago."

Jason didn't smile back at the weak attempt at humor. "I'm not interested in the china. I'm interested in what the hell happened to my parents' marriage."

Kevin sighed, a bone-deep weariness stealing through him. "Son, if I knew that, maybe I could make it right."

When Jason started to probe more deeply, Kevin shook his head. "I will not talk about this," he warned with quiet finality. "Go home to your wife. She's expecting your baby. She needs you there."

"The baby's not due for another three months. I hardly think Dana's desperate for me to get home and watch her as if she might break. Besides, every time she gets the least little bit queasy, so do I. We're running out of crackers."

"Then buy some and go home," Kevin said flatly.

This time it was Jason who sighed. "Okay, but if you need to talk, Dad..."

Kevin might not be able to explain what had happened, or his own feelings, but he couldn't ignore the pain and confusion in Jason's tone. He relented as much as he could. "I'll come looking for you, son. I promise."

Finally, after several endless minutes, Jason nodded, his expression resigned. He stood in the doorway and said, "If you want her back, Dad, you're going to have to fight for her."

"I know that." What he didn't say was that he wasn't at all sure he had the energy left for the battle.

Jason left finally, shutting the office door very quietly behind him.

That careful exit, more than anything, told Kevin just how upset his son was. Jason slammed doors. From the time he'd been able to walk, he'd raced through life, hitting doors at full tilt, letting them crash behind him. The quiet closing of Kevin's door with its implied hint of defeat was just one more sign that both of their worlds had suddenly gone topsyturvy.

When Jason had gone, Kevin leaned back in his chair and wondered why it had taken a crisis of this magnitude to begin to open the lines of communication with his son. If nothing else came from this damnable separation, at least perhaps he would have the new bond that had formed over the last few months between him and Jason.

After years of distance and a sense that they never connected, Kevin had been stunned to realize that his son truly did love him. It had been equally surprising to realize that Jason had matured so much. Kevin gave Dana a lot of credit for that. She had given Jason a sense of direction. Besides that, his daughter-in-law was every bit as determined as Lacey had once been to see that the Halloran family ties remained close-knit.

Jason, Dana, even Kevin's father used every opportunity to try to push him into reconciling with his wife. Right now, though, Kevin wasn't up to explaining that the choice wasn't his. He couldn't cope with explanations, period. The fact of the matter was that he couldn't cope with anything these days. There was an aching, leaden sensation in the middle of his chest that never seemed to go away.

If Jason didn't understand his separation from Lacey, it was a thousand times worse for him. How could a love that had begun in the fifth grade, a marriage that had lasted over twenty-five years, fall apart in a split second?

The day a year earlier when Lacey had moved out of their huge house and into a tiny apartment of her own, Kevin had been stunned. Sure, they'd had a few fights. She couldn't seem to understand the demands of running a business like Halloran Industries. In her own quiet way she had badgered him to let up, to spend more time with her, to think of his health.

The next thing he knew, Lacey was forcing his hand, trying to recapture a time long ago, a time when, as he saw it now, he'd avoided responsibility, rather than accepting it. Her harsh all-or-nothing ultimatum— Halloran Industries or a marriage—had taken him by surprise. His inability to make the decision she'd demanded had been answer enough, it seemed. In her view, with his silence, he had chosen the generations-old family textile business over her.

Lacey had made good on her threat, too. Kevin didn't have to understand her decision to know that it was final. Lacey appeared easygoing and flexible, but beneath that gentle facade was a stubborn streak a mile wide. He'd recognized it the first time he'd seen the defiant lift of her chin, despite the sheen of tears in her eleven-year-old eyes. That fierce determination, that willingness to spit in the eye of her own fears had made her a perfect match for a Halloran.

It was up to Lacey to explain her moving out to Jason, though. Kevin wasn't about to try. He would never be able to hide his anger or this raw, gut-wrenching feeling of utter helplessness that was totally alien to him. He might understand the most intricate details of business administration, but over the past year he'd come to realize he didn't know a damn thing about women, not even the one woman who'd captured his heart so very long ago.

And, to his profound regret given the circumstances, the woman who held it still.

"Mom, I just don't get it. What happened? Why did you move out? I thought you'd go back long ago. Haven't you made your point yet?"

How many times was Jason going to ask her that? Lacey Halloran wondered. How many times would she have to give the same stupid, evasive answer because she couldn't bear to get into the truth?

"Jason, that is between your father and me," she said, her tone gentle as she busied herself repotting a bright red geranium to keep her son from seeing how her hands shook. It wouldn't do at all for him to see how much she feared the empty days ahead, an emptiness she had brought on herself.

Lacey couldn't blame Jason for being confused. She'd felt that way herself for months now, maybe even years. She'd felt her relationship with Kevin sliding not just into a rut, but into some deep, dark ravine. Finally she couldn't take it any longer, couldn't bury the memories of the dear, rebellious young man who'd set himself up as her protector when they'd been barely eleven.

In those days Kevin had been noble and brave and adventurous. They'd roared through the sixties with spirit and love and idealism. Even now she wasn't sure exactly when he'd started to change or when she'd first noticed the shift in priorities, the abandonment of values they'd once shared.

Maybe it was when he'd caved in to pressure from his father to join Halloran Industries. Brandon had used every trick in the book to lure his son into taking his rightful place in the family business. He'd finally played on Kevin's guilt, convincing him that he was doing a disservice to his wife and son by not giving them everything they deserved. None of Lacey's protests had been able to allay Kevin's fear that his father was right.

Maybe it was after that, when he'd ignored her open distaste and bought that huge, monstrous house that was more like a mausoleum than a home. Kevin had wanted a place suitable for entertaining business associates, a palace for her, he'd said. Brandon's realtor had taken them to showcases. Ironically, Kevin had chosen the one most similar to the lonely status symbol of a house in which he'd been raised himself.

There were other symptoms of the chasm widening between them. Determined to prove himself, to exceed Brandon's high expectations, he'd begun spending longer and longer hours at the office. Lacey had even suspected, but never proven, that he was having an affair.

There were desperate times when she even pinpointed something as silly and unimportant as the moment when he'd traded folk songs and rock for classical music as an indication of all that was going wrong with their marriage.

Somewhere along the way, though, the life she'd anticipated with Kevin had changed. She had never expected to be caught up in a whirlwind of social, business and charitable demands. She had never expected to see Kevin's decency and strength lost to ambition.

As CEO of Halloran Industries, Kevin had become a respected member of Boston's elite establishment. But ideals they had once cherished, dreams they had worked for together, had been lost. Worst of all, Kevin seemed blind to the significance of the changes and the destruction of all they once held dear.

In the heat of that last, bitter argument, he had accused her of not keeping pace, of being unwilling to change, unable to accept the reality of getting ahead in a world that respected nothing so much as success.

If that was a flaw, so be it, Lacey thought, angrily snapping off a dead geranium leaf. What was so terrible about wanting to help others? Wanting to make a home for her family?

Wanting a husband to stop killing himself?

She sighed. Was there anything more important than love and family and commitment? It might be old-fashioned, but dammit she would fight to her dying breath to preserve those simple ideals, to get her husband to wake up before it was too late. She wanted that special, wonderful man she'd loved for so terribly long back again.

Even so, even though it had broken her heart to watch his rare, generous spirit wither and die, she might have forced herself to accept the changes if only Kevin had seemed happy. In lives otherwise rich with love, she might have accepted that no one ever stayed the same, if only his complexion hadn't taken on that deathly pallor.

Instead of being happy and energetic, he'd merely seemed driven. The effect on his health was devastating. He'd already suffered one heart attack, a mild one that the doctor described as a warning.

Rather than modifying his life-style, though, Kevin had become even more obsessed. They had argued again and again. Lacey had pleaded with him to stop killing himself, for him to at least try to make her see why he felt so driven. His response had been to avoid the arguments by spending even longer hours at the office. There had been one last explosive argument and then she had gone, unable to bear even one more day of watching him die before her eyes, one more lonely evening waiting for a call from some hospital emergency room.

Lacey couldn't say all that to Jason, though. He hadn't even been married an entire year yet himself. How could a mother explain the tarnish that eventually robbed love of its shine to a man for whom it still held a shimmering beauty? Instead she deliberately asked about Dana and watched his expression soften, heard the warmth steal back into his voice, replacing the despair that had been evident only moments before.

"Dana's glowing," he said. "She considers this pregnancy the grandest adventure in her life. Quite a statement given her decision to raise her brother on her own."

Lacey chuckled. "It certainly is an adventure. You're both happy about it, then? I wondered. It seemed a little soon. You have so many adjustments to make, especially with her brother living with you."

"To my astonishment, Sammy is no trouble at all. He spends every spare second with Granddad. The other night I found them crawling around under one of the looms at the plant. Granddad was trying to explain how to get a white-on-white pattern on damask."

"Does Sammy even know what damask is?" Lacey asked, trying to imagine the sixteen-year-old hell-raiser with the outrageous haircut being familiar with fine fabrics.

"Actually that's how the subject came up in the first place, as I understand it. Sammy wanted to use Granddad's tablecloth for a ghost costume for some play."

The image brought a smile to her lips. "I can just imagine Brandon's reaction to that."

Jason shook his head. "No, you can't. He actually got the scissors for him. But before he'd let Sammy ruin the tablecloth, he insisted on showing him how it was made. Off they went to the plant, leaving dinner still sitting on the table. Needless to say, Sammy changed his mind once he saw that the cloth wasn't some old rag Granddad had gotten from a discount store."

Lacey tapped the soil gently around the geranium's roots, then put the pot aside and reached for another. The rich scent of earth and the pungent aroma of the flowers had begun to work their soothing magic. She could almost forget her life was no longer complete.

"I saw Dad last night," Jason said, all the laughter gone from his voice, replaced by a cautious note.

Lacey drew in a deep breath. Her hands stilled. The announcement brought a shuddering end to her tranquility. "How is he?" she asked finally.

"Terrible, though he won't admit it. Mom, you still love him. I can see that. And he's still crazy about you. How long are the two of you going to let this go on?"

"As long as it takes."

"As long as it takes to do what?" Jason demanded, his tone filled with frustration. "Do either of you have the faintest idea why you're apart?"

"We're apart because that's the way it has to be."

Before she could stop him, Jason crushed the bright red petals of a geranium between his fingers. She wasn't even sure he was aware of what he'd done until he glanced down. Then he impatiently tossed the mangled bloom aside.

"That doesn't make a damned bit of sense," he said, raking his fingers through blond hair the same shade his father's had been at that age.

"Stop." Lacey put her hand over his.

"Are you trying to find yourself? Is that what this is? Some crazy mid-life crisis?"

Lacey drew in a deep breath. "I couldn't watch it anymore," she admitted quietly, giving in to Jason's desperate need to understand something that was almost beyond explaining. "I couldn't sit by and watch your father destroy his health. I was dying bit by bit, right along with him. I tried everything I knew, but nothing worked."

Her son stared at her, his eyes filled with astonishment. "Are you saying that you wanted to shock him into letting up?"

Tears misted in her eyes. She blinked them away. "I hoped that our marriage would matter enough, that *I* would matter enough, to make him stop killing himself."

"But you *are* the only thing that matters to him."

She shook her head. "Not anymore. Not enough. Have you seen any signs that he's changing? Admit it, since I left, he's only working harder."

"Because he has no reason to go home. Don't you see? You've created a catch-22."

"So what should I do? Go home and watch him die? Give him permission to do it? I won't do that, Jason. I can't."

"Can't you talk about it? Compromise?"

"Not about this."

Jason ran his fingers through his hair again in the gesture he'd picked up from his wife. "Damn! What an awful mess."

"I'm sorry. I'm sorry you're caught in the middle. I would give anything for that not to be."

"I love you both. I want to see you happy again, the way you used to be."

Lacey's lips curved into a rueful smile. "No one wants that any more than I do. I promise you that."

They were still talking when the phone rang. Lacey picked it up and heard a cool, impersonal voice inform her that Kevin Halloran had just been brought into the hospital. "He's in the cardiac intensive care unit. He wanted you to know."

"Oh, God," she whispered softly, sinking into a chair, her own heart pounding.

"Mom, what is it? Is it Granddad? Dad?"

"Your father," she said, taking his hand, needing his strength to ask into the phone, "How is he? Will he make it?"

"His condition is critical."

Leaving had accomplished nothing, Lacey thought bitterly. Nothing.

Then, with a rush of panic, she tried to bring herself to face the very real possibility of losing forever the man she had loved nearly her whole life.

Chapter Two

The ten-mile ride across town to the hospital was the longest Lacey had ever taken, even though Jason drove like a maniac. His expression was grim, and she was certain she'd detected accusation in his eyes from the moment she'd told him about his father's heart attack. Whatever he thought, it was no worse than what she was mentally telling herself. She felt as if the guilt were smothering her.

The deep sadness, the sense of magic lost that had pervaded her entire being for so long had vanished in the brief seconds of that phone call, replaced by a gut-wrenching fear. Kevin couldn't die, not like this, not with so very much between them unresolved.

"It's my fault," she said when she could stand the silence no longer. "I moved out. Maybe if I'd stayed..." But she knew deep down it wouldn't have mattered. Kevin had made up his mind to tempt fate.

And he'd lost. Dear God, she prayed, don't let him pay with his life. Make this just one more warning. Give him one more chance.

Jason glanced her way. "He's going to be okay, Mother. Stop beating yourself up over this. Casting blame isn't going to do Dad any good. Did the hospital call Granddad?"

She realized she hadn't asked, that she had no idea where Kevin had been when he'd had the heart attack or even how he'd gotten to the hospital. "I don't know. I don't know any more than what I've told you."

"Maybe Granddad was with him. Knowing the two of them, they were probably still at the office."

Jason seemed to take comfort from the possibility that Brandon had been with Kevin, that he might even now be with him. Lacey was less certain how she felt about seeing her father-in-law. She dreaded another confrontation. They'd already had one monumental set-to over her decision to move out.

Brandon had ranted and raved, even questioned her sanity. She knew it killed him that he couldn't manipulate them all like puppets on a string. She wasn't sure she could stand another meeting like that, especially tonight.

The bottom line, though, was that in his own way Brandon loved Kevin every bit as much as she did and wanted what was best for him. Unfortunately, they tended to differ on what that was.

Despite their differences, he had every right to be at Kevin's side. Knowing Brandon, though, he would figure he had more of a right to be there than she did. Maybe that was true. She didn't know anymore.

"It's my fault," she said again as Jason sped into the parking lot by the emergency entrance and screeched to a halt in the first space he could find.

"Stop it," Jason said impatiently, slamming the car door and coming around to join her. "You did what you thought you had to do. I may not agree with your methods, but I know you did it out of love."

"Maybe I did it out of selfishness," she countered and bit back a sob as guilt clogged her throat. "Maybe I was only thinking of my needs, not his."

"You don't have a selfish bone in your body," Jason said, taking her by the shoulders and giving her a gentle shake. He scanned her face. "Are you going to be okay?"

Lacey drew in a deep breath. She slowly, consciously pulled herself together and gave him a tremulous smile. "I'm not the one in intensive care. I'll be fine." She took his hand. "Let's go see your father."

Upstairs they found Brandon Halloran pacing the long, empty corridor outside of cardiac intensive care. Not even he could bluster his way past the restricted visiting hours posted on the door. Pale and shaken, his expression was bleak as he waited for word on his son's condition.

Jason put an arm around his grandfather's shoulders and steered him toward the waiting room, but Lacey held back, uncertain of Brandon's mood.

Years ago, before she and Kevin had even married, they had been the closest thing to enemies. Brandon had blamed her for so much that was wrong with his relationship with his son. Since then they'd forged a cautious friendship, which appeared to have splintered into a million pieces because she'd abandoned his beloved and only son.

Hesitant, Lacey stood in the doorway of the waiting room until Brandon held out his hand. Then she moved quickly, anxious for news, anxious for a little of Brandon's towering, unshakable strength. Clasping his firm but icy hand between her own, she asked, "How is he? What have they told you?"

"Not a damned thing," he grumbled. "As much money as I give to this place, you'd think I could get a straight answer out of someone."

"What happened?"

A shadow seemed to pass over his eyes as he remembered. "Found him at his desk, all slumped over.

Thought for a minute he might be dead. The guard got the paramedics there and we brought him here.''

"Was he conscious?" Lacey asked.

"Part of the time. Said he wanted to see you. I don't pretend to understand what's been wrong between the two of you, but I want you to put it aside for now," he said, giving her a warning look that Lacey recognized from a dozen different occasions.

Brandon Halloran had strong opinions on family loyalty and just about everything else. He wasn't afraid to voice them. He had the confidence of a man who'd done well with his life and knew it. In fact, he thought the world would be a whole lot better if everyone would just accept the wisdom of his plans for them. It had galled the daylights out of him that Lacey and Kevin had dared to go their own way, at least in the beginning.

As much as she might have resented it once, Lacey found there was something almost comforting about the familiarity of his response to this crisis. That strength of purpose, that single-minded clarity of vision was welcome tonight in a way it never had been before. If there was any way in hell Brandon Halloran could buy salvation for his son, he would do it.

"I do love him," she said gently. "That's never been the problem."

Brandon scowled at her. "Well, I'll be damned if I know what is. I listened to all that double-talk you gave me months ago, chewed it over in my head every second since then and, by God, I still can't make a bit of sense of it. You got some sort of complaint about the life-style he gave you?''

"No," she whispered, stung by the harsh accusation. "Not the way you mean."

"I didn't notice you turning down the house, that fancy sports car."

Little did he know how she had fought both, Lacey thought but refused to say. Kevin had insisted. Brandon would never believe that, though. Even at the best of times in Brandon and Lacey's tenuous relationship, she'd been very much aware that he expected the worst of her, that he didn't entirely understand that someone could be motivated by something other than money and status, especially someone who'd brought nothing more than the strength of her love to a marriage.

"What then?" he demanded roughly. "Make me see why a woman would walk out on a man who's provided her with everything money could buy."

"I only wanted my husband back," she told him, but she could see that Brandon couldn't fathom what she meant. He started to speak, but Jason cut him off.

"Granddad," he said, "this isn't the time."

The fight seemed to drain out of Brandon as quickly as it had stirred. "No. No, it's not." It was the closest he was likely to come to an apology. He asked Jason, "You called Dana yet?"

Jason shook his head. "I don't want to upset her."

"She'd want to be here," Lacey told him. "Go call. We'll be okay."

With Jason gone, the look she and Brandon exchanged was measuring. She suspected he was trying every bit as hard as she was to avoid starting another pointless argument. But the only way around it was small talk or silence. She didn't have the stomach for small talk. Neither, she suspected, did he.

"Damn, I hate this waiting," he said finally. "You want some coffee or something?"

Lacey shook her head. "Nothing."

"How do you suppose he ended up in a fix like this? He's a young man yet."

"It's not the first time," she reminded him. "If anything, he took worse care of himself after the first attack."

"And I suppose you're blaming that on me."

"Casting blame won't help," she said, repeating what Jason had said to try to comfort her. It didn't work on Brandon, either. He took up his impatient pacing again.

If someone didn't come out and talk to them soon, Brandon was likely to call up the hospital board's president and demand a change in administration, she thought. He'd wave another endowment under the president's nose for effect. Waiting was always hardest on a man who was used to making things happen.

Lacey hated it, too, because it gave her time to think, time to remember the way it had once been between her and Kevin, back at the very beginning.

It had been her first day at a new school. Worse, it was the middle of the year. Friendships had been made and she was an outsider. She was eleven years old, tall, skinny, shy and awkward.

She had been so sure that the other kids would make fun of her, that they would see that the clothes she wore were hand-me-downs, that her hair had been clipped impatiently by her mother, rather than in some fancy salon. She was terrified that they would discover that her last classmates had labeled her a brain and left her out of anything fun.

It had taken every ounce of bravery she'd possessed to slip into the classroom and scurry to a seat in the back, hoping no one would notice her. Then the teacher had singled her out, introduced her as a newcomer and made her move right smack to the middle of a room in which students had been seated in alphabetical order. She'd felt all those inquisitive, judgmental eyes on her and she'd wanted to cry.

She'd rushed too fast, trying to slide into her assigned seat without anyone taking further notice of her. Instead, she'd spilled her books in the process and had to listen to the taunting laughter that had made her feel more an outsider than ever. She'd kept her chin up, but hadn't been able to stop the tears from filling her eyes. She'd desperately tried to blink them away before anyone saw.

But a boy with tousled golden hair and a smile that revealed a chipped front tooth had seen. He had knelt down, picked up the books and placed them on her desk.

"Thank you, Kevin," Mrs. Niles had said, while the other boys in the room had made wisecracks about his gallantry.

Lacey had felt awful, knowing that he'd been embarrassed in front of his friends just for coming to her rescue. She had given him a hesitant smile and felt her eleven-year-old heart tumble at the impish, unworried grin he shot her in return.

From that moment on Kevin Halloran had been her protector, her knight in shining armor. He'd withstood a lot of teasing for befriending her. He'd fought a lot of playground battles on her behalf, had chosen her for teams when others wouldn't, had badgered her to try out for cheerleading when she'd known she wasn't pretty enough or popular enough to make it. To her amazement, he'd been right. She had cheered loudest and longest when he'd raced for the goal line.

Later, he'd ignored a lot of wealthy, admiring teenaged girls to date her, apparently preferring their quiet, serious talks to the adolescent wiles of her peers.

Then he'd dared to fall in love with her.

Brandon Halloran had thrown one of his inimitable fits about the engagement. He'd declared that no son of his was going to marry some little nobody who was only after his money. He'd vowed to do everything in his power to see that they split up. In the lowest moment of her life, he had offered her a bribe. When that hadn't worked, he'd sent Kevin off to college at Stanford, hoping that distance would accomplish what his ranting and threats had not.

None of it had dimmed Kevin and Lacey's determination or their love. Sometimes it astonished Lacey that at that age they had stood firm against the power of Brandon's opposition. In anyone else it might have been sheer stubbornness, but with Kevin it had been a deeply ingrained conviction that Lacey brought something into his life that he could never hope to find with another woman. At least that's what he'd told her when he'd insisted that they would get married with or without his parents' approval. He'd defiantly exchanged his class ring for a tiny chip of a diamond, rather than use parental funds for something splashier.

Where had that steadfast sense of commitment gone? The love hadn't died. As she sat in a corner of the cold, dimly lit hospital waiting room, terrified of losing him forever this time, Lacey could admit that much. She also knew that they couldn't go on as they had been, drifting farther and farther apart with each day that passed, fighting bitterly at every turn.

Jason returned just as Dr. Lincoln Westlake came out of the cardiac unit. Lacey froze at the sight of his grim expression. Even Brandon looked uncertain. It was Jason who finally dared to ask how Kevin was doing.

"I won't lie to you. He's in pretty bad shape. If I had to guess, I'd say he didn't take that last attack seriously and did everything in his power to ensure he'd have another one."

Brandon gazed at him in astonishment. "Are you saying he tried to bring this on?"

"In a way."

"That's absurd. Why that would be the next best thing to suicide."

"Mr. Halloran, your son is a bright man. He knew the risks and he did nothing to minimize them." He glanced at Lacey, and his tone gentled. "Did he?"

She sighed. The truth was that he'd even canceled half a dozen follow-up appointments with the doctor. She'd finally given up trying to make them.

"No. Nothing," she admitted. Damn him, she said to herself. Damn Kevin Halloran for trying to play God with his own life!

"Can I see him?" she asked, when she could keep her voice steady.

"For five minutes. He's resting now and I don't want you to wake him. If he's to have any chance at all, he needs to stay as quiet as possible."

Lacey nodded. "Thanks, Linc. If anyone can pull him through this, I know you can."

"I'm going to do my damnedest. If he'll give me a little help, we might have a chance. You come on in, when you're ready."

As he walked away, Lacey started toward the cardiac unit after him. Brandon stepped into her path. "Remember what the doctor said, girl. Don't you go upsetting him!"

"Granddad!" Jason warned.

Lacey put her hand on her son's arm. "It's okay." She met Brandon's gaze evenly and saw the worry and exhaustion in his eyes. "I'll tell him that you're here and that you're praying for him."

Brandon nodded, then sighed heavily and sank into one of the cushioned chairs. He motioned for Jason to sit next to him, then looked up at her. "You tell him we're all praying for him," he said.

Lacey nodded. She pressed the button that allowed the automatic doors to the unit to swish silently open, then stepped into a high-tech wonderland that was both magnificent and frightening.

Like the spokes of a wheel, small, softly lit rooms surrounded a central desk banked with monitors.

Hushed voices competed with beeping equipment and the steady gurgle of oxygen.

She spotted Linc through one of the doorways, a chart in his hand, his troubled gaze riveted on the bed. Drawing in a deep breath, she walked to the doorway. Linc gave her a reassuring smile and motioned her in. Her steps were halting, but she finally approached the bed.

It took every last ounce of her courage to glance past the tangle of wires, IV tubes and oxygen to her husband.

Against the startling white of the pillow, Kevin's handsome, angular face had a grayish cast. His golden hair, shot now with silver, was mussed, its impeccable cut wasted. Without the armor of his custom-tailored suit, his designer shirt and silk tie, he looked vulnerable, every inch a mortal, rather than the invincible hero she'd always thought him to be.

He was so terribly still, she thought, fighting panic. The man who had always seemed so alive, so filled with energy looked like a shadow, quiet and lifeless. Her gaze shifted desperately to a monitor and fixed on the steady rhythm. She had no idea what the up-and-down movement of the lines meant except that they were proof her husband was still clinging to life.

Lacey stepped closer and took Kevin's one free hand, curving her fingers around his, trying to share her warmth with him. Her own heart lurched anew at his vulnerability, then filled to overflowing, first with love, then with rage—at him and at her own impotence.

Damn you, Kevin, she thought. *You were always my strength. I'm not sure I know how to be yours.*

She whispered, "Fight, Kevin. Dammit, you have to live. You have a grandchild on the way. You have to be here to teach him how to ride a bicycle, how to throw a ball. You know I'm not good at things like that."

She closed her eyes and thought of all the plans they'd made. She kept her voice low as she reminded him, willed him to live to see them come true.

"Don't you remember how we always looked forward to spoiling our grandchildren? There were so many things we were going to do. We were going to spend long, lazy days walking on the beach. We were going to read Shakespeare's sonnets and visit Walden Pond. Don't you dare make me do those things alone."

She felt Linc's hand on her shoulder. "That's enough for now," he said gently. "Let him rest."

"Not yet," she pleaded, terrified Kevin would slip away if she weren't there to hold on to him. "Another minute, please. I won't say another word. Just let me stay."

Linc studied her silently, then nodded. He reached for a tissue and handed it to her. "Another minute," he agreed. "No more."

Lacey brushed away the tears she hadn't even real-ized were there until she had the tissue in her hand. Very much aware of her vow to remain silent, she tried bargaining in her mind with Kevin and then with God.

With her gaze riveted on her husband's face, she was aware of the first subtle blink of his lashes. Hope burst inside her. That's it, she cried in her heart. You can do it, Kevin. I know you can.

She knew her minute's reprieve was long over, but she didn't budge, waiting. It was a minute more and then another before Kevin's eyes finally blinked open and his gaze searched the room before finally focus-ing on her.

He managed a feeble smile that was only a faint shadow of the smile that had captivated her heart all those years ago. Even so, Lacey's heart filled to bursting and she felt tears of relief spill down her cheeks. In that instant she knew beyond a doubt that whatever it took, her husband was going to make it. He would fight to live.

But the struggle to save their marriage was yet to come.

Chapter Three

Lacey spent a long, uneasy night in the hospital waiting room, refusing to go home, desperately needing the few precious minutes every couple of hours that Linc allowed her to visit Kevin. She couldn't rid herself of that first sense of shock at his pallor, that initial horror that he might give up and slip away. Fear welled up inside her and abated only when she was by his side, willing her strength into him.

It had been nearly midnight when she had insisted that Jason take Dana home. She tried futilely to get Brandon to go with them. She was worried about the exhaustion that had shadowed his eyes. It reminded her all too vividly of those first grief-stricken weeks after he had lost his wife. For all that Brandon thought otherwise, he was not invincible.

Now, even though he was resting, he looked miserably uncomfortable on the waiting room's too-short sofa. Lacey couldn't help thinking he would have been far better off in his own bed, in his own home with Mrs. Farnsworth, his housekeeper of thirty years, fussing over him. Still, she could understand his need to stay close to Kevin. Despite all she and Kevin had been through lately—all the bitterness and recriminations—she'd felt the same way.

Though Kevin hadn't awakened again through the long night, Lacey had been comforted simply by seeing him, by listening to the steady sound of the monitor tracking his heartbeat. Now, her throat dry, her stomach growling, she went off in search of tea and toast for herself and her father-in-law. If Brandon was going to insist on staying until the crisis passed, he would need all his strength.

Brandon was awake when Lacey returned, his cheek bearing the pattern of the sofa's piping, his clothes rumpled to a state that would have given his personal tailor palpitations. His eyes were brighter, though.

"Wondered where you'd gone," he said, accepting the cup of tea and ignoring the toast.

Even in this crisis he obviously had no intention of veering from his Spartan routine, Lacey thought with a mix of admiration and frustration. No wonder Kevin found his father such a tough act to follow.

"The doctor was by a minute ago," he said, interrupting her thoughts. "Can't believe that boy who used to climb trees in my backyard is a cardiologist these days. You suppose we ought to call in someone else?"

"Linc is one of the best and you know it."

"I suppose." He still looked doubtful.

"What did he say?"

"He thinks the worst is past. If Kevin stays stable another forty-eight hours, he'll consider moving him to a private room."

"And then what?" she asked, more to herself than Brandon.

His sharp gaze pinned her, the blue eyes glinting with a challenge. "Then we'll all do whatever it takes to help Kevin get his health back. All of us, you hear me?"

Lacey shook her head ruefully. An order like that was all too typical of her father-in-law. "Brandon, you can't bully us into a happy marriage."

He scowled and waved a finger under her nose. "Maybe not, but I can damn well see that you stick it out until this crisis is past."

Determined not to let him see how his threat disturbed her, Lacey returned his fierce expression.

"I will not argue with you about this," she said, carefully setting her tea on the table, then turning and walking away. Maybe it was the cowardly thing to do, but she couldn't see any other choice. The stress of the present on both of them was bad enough without battling over the future.

Outside the hospital, where winter hadn't quite given way to spring, a bed of purple crocuses were forcing their way through the still-icy earth. Lacey circled the grounds, holding her thin jacket closed against the damp breeze. The nip in the air cleared her head. She reminded herself that for all his blustering, Brandon couldn't control whatever decision she and Kevin reached about their marriage.

That decision, however, was far in the future. Brandon was right about one thing: the most important task now was to see that Kevin pulled through, that he took this latest warning more seriously than he had the last. She, more than anyone, wanted to see his masculine vitality restored, to see his pallor replaced by the healthy glow he'd once had.

She recalled the way he'd looked on their wedding day, his hair too long by his father's standards and tousled by a spring breeze. Used to seeing him in jeans and denim jackets, she'd thought he looked outrageously sexy and impressive in custom-tailored gray slacks and a blue dress shirt. She'd never guessed he owned clothes like that, though it stood to reason he would, given the family's business in textiles and their social standing. Usually, though, Kevin had rebelled at anything that hinted at his privileged background.

Most of all, Lacey recalled the expression of adoration on his face when she'd joined him on that blustery hillside. She had been so proud to become his wife, so touched by the tender vows he'd written himself. The emotions she had felt that day had only deepened with time. In the end she had loved him enough to leave, loved him enough to risk everything she cared about on the one slim chance that the desperate measure would force him to face the dangers of his present life-style.

Steeped in bittersweet memories, Lacey walked until it was time to go back in to see Kevin. She avoided the waiting room and Brandon, going instead straight to the cardiac unit.

She found Kevin with his eyes closed, his expression more peaceful. His jaw was shadowed by the first faint stubble of a beard that under other circumstances she might have found sexy because of its ruggedly sensual look. It would have reminded her of the rebellious, bearded young man who'd marched for peace at a time when his father was backing the Vietnam War. Today it only reminded her of how sick he was, because that shadow emphasized his pallor.

Seated by his bed, his hand in hers, Lacey's thoughts began drifting back again. She was startled when she heard him whisper her name.

"Lacey, is that you?"

"It's me, Kevin."

"You stayed," he said, gently squeezing her hand. He sounded surprised.

"I stayed," she murmured, then added wearily, "but dammit, Kevin Halloran, did you have to go to this extreme just to get my attention?"

"You're here, aren't you?" he responded with that familiar teasing note in his weakened voice. His tone sobered. "What's Linc saying?"

"He says you're going to be all right, if you take care of yourself and slow down."

A faint twinkle sparked in his eyes as his gaze met hers. "Sounds like a fate worse than death."

"Don't you dare joke about it," she said furiously, jerking her hand from his and poking it into her pocket. "You scared the daylights out of all of us."

"Does Jason know? He came to see me at the office. Was it last night? Or before? I've lost track of the time."

"It was two nights ago. He came to see me last night. He was with me when the hospital called."

"I'm afraid we had words."

"So he mentioned. He's frustrated and confused. He wants to help, but he doesn't know how."

Kevin sighed heavily. "That makes two of us."

Lacey bit back a retort that would match the faint edge of bitterness in his. If she started saying all that was on her mind—the whole jumble of fury and regrets—Linc would throw her out of intensive care.

"Lace?"

She met Kevin's troubled gaze. "Yes."

"You haven't forgiven me, have you?"

Faced with that unblinking, uncompromising stare, she could only shake her head. Instead of saying more, she deliberately changed the subject.

"Your father is outside. He's been here all night. In fact, he was driving the staff crazy because he had to wait to find out what was going on. I think he thought he ought to be in here telling them how to get the oxygen started."

Lacey waited for Kevin's familiar grinning response to tales of his father's efforts to manage life on his terms. Instead he winced. Lacey caught his effort to hide it and asked, "Are you in pain? Should I call the nurse?"

He grimaced. "I feel as if I've been run over by a truck."

"You look like it, too."

He reached for her hand again and when she finally placed it in his, he held on tight. "You were right, weren't you, Lace?"

"About what?"

"The work. I got my priorities all screwed up."

Lacey hadn't wanted to wring an admission from Kevin like this. Besides, the truth of the matter was that work was only part of the problem. Worse was the fact that the man who'd been her lover and best friend had too often seemed little more than a stranger.

"Now's not the time to talk about that," she told him.

"Can we talk about it, though?" he said, a sense of urgency in his voice.

"I always thought we could talk about anything," she replied softly, unable to hide the regret.

Blue eyes pinned her. "Until I shut you out," he said.

"I never said that."

"But it's the truth. I did. I'm sorry."

"Kevin—"

"I want us to start over. When I get out of here, I want to go away, take a long vacation and make things right between us again. I've missed you these past months, more than I can say." His voice faltered. "I just . . . I wanted you to know."

When she didn't say a word, couldn't squeeze a sound around the tears that clogged her throat, he prodded, "Lace, what do you think? Can we give it a try?"

A part of her thought it was too late. A part of her wanted to scream that this sudden change of attitude was too easy, a quick reaction to a health crisis that would pass as soon as he felt more like himself again.

And yet a part of her yearned for the way it used to be between them, wanted to believe it was possible to recapture the richness of their love.

"We'll talk about it when you're out of here," she said evasively.

Every bit as stubborn as his father, Kevin wouldn't let it go that easily. "You won't back out?"

Lacey drew in a deep breath and met his gaze evenly. "Of talking?" she asked. "No. I won't back out."

Kevin sighed then, obviously content with that much of a commitment. His eyes slowly drifted closed. He was still clinging to her hand, the touch apparently as much comfort for him as it was for her.

Kevin knew he was going to have a fight on his hands. He'd seen that much in Lacey's brilliant blue eyes, even when she'd reluctantly agreed to talk about the future. For some reason a fight didn't scare him anymore, not half as much as the thought of losing her forever.

Besides, nothing about his relationship with Lacey had ever been easy, not from the day he'd told his parents about her, anyway. Before that, they had spent long, quiet hours talking, sharing innermost thoughts that no boy dared to share with his buddies. Lacey's gentle smiles had brought sunshine into his life from the day they'd met.

More than simply his friend, she was his social conscience. She was the first person to make him realize that not everyone was as fortunate as he was, that he had an obligation to look beyond his own narrow world. From the first moment she had looked at him like a hero, he'd wanted to prove himself worthy of her.

Then Brandon had started throwing his weight around, threatening Lacey, scowling at Kevin, swearing that the Halloran name would be sullied forever if he dared to marry a woman lacking the requisite Boston pedigree.

The truth of the matter was that Brandon had been afraid. He'd spent his whole life making plans for the day when Kevin would take his rightful place at Halloran Industries. But Kevin hadn't been interested. Brandon had blamed Lacey for that. He'd accused her of ruining his son's life, of forcing him to choose between her and his heritage.

Infuriated by the unjust accusation, Lacey had faced Brandon down, her shoulders squared, her chin jutting out, her eyes filled with fire. Only her hands, clenched at her sides, gave away her nervousness.

Her voice steady, she had said, "You're the one making him choose. I want Kevin to be happy. If Halloran Industries makes him happy, it's fine with me. But he says he wants to do something else with his life.''

Kevin had never been more proud of her. Brandon had appeared stunned by her spunk and by her blunt words. He'd turned to Kevin. ''Is what she's saying right? You don't want to work with me?''

''It's not that, Dad. You think of Halloran Industries as some sort of family dynasty. I need to prove myself. I don't want something that's handed to me.''

''You're just one of those damned hippies. Just look at you. Your hair's too long. You dress like a bum.''

''I dress like everyone else.''

''Not like everyone else in *this* family,'' Brandon said in disgust. ''You think we should be ashamed of having money. Well, dammit, I worked for every penny we have. So did your granddad, and you will, too.''

''You're acting as if clothes are the only things that matter. What about having a social conscience? Doesn't that matter at all to you?''

Brandon slammed his fist down on his desk. ''You act as if you invented it. You'll have to work for what you get at Halloran, same as I did. And you'll be expected to share with the community, the same way I have, the way your granddad did.''

''It won't be the same and you know it. You think writing a check covers you for all eternity. What about fighting for what's right, fighting to make a difference? That's what I care about. That's what I want to do with my life. I just can't see myself making fancy fabrics for the wealthy when people are going hungry."

"And what about the people who have food on their tables every night because we provide them with jobs? You think that doesn't count for anything?"

Kevin had been at a loss to argue that point. Somehow he'd been so certain back then that he could find ways to make his life count, to better things for thousands, rather than the mere hundred or so employed by Halloran Industries.

Lacey had stood by him when he'd walked away from the Halloran money, turned his back on his family. As he remembered, he thought perhaps those were the best years of their lives. They had struggled. At times they hadn't had two nickels to rub together, but it had been okay because they'd had dreams and they'd had each other.

They'd worked side by side to help people who didn't have nearly as much, people who didn't believe in themselves.

Educated in business and drawn by an idealistic notion of making the world a better place, Kevin had applied his skills in a series of low-paying and off-times unrewarding public service jobs. For several years he found the sacrifices he made worthwhile. He was filled with satisfaction and hope. He'd never once been tempted to touch his trust fund for himself.

Then he'd realized that for every instance in which he made a difference, there were a dozen more about which he could do nothing. Increasingly frustrated after nearly fifteen years of struggling, he was finally ready to listen when his father pressed him yet again about joining Halloran Industries.

It hadn't been difficult for Kevin to justify his eventual acceptance of the offer. Perhaps from a position of power, he would be able to make the changes in society that up to now had eluded him. And, as Brandon pointed out with distressing accuracy, his beautiful Lacey and his wonderful son did not deserve to live like paupers just so Kevin could make some obviously misguided political statement.

Like so many other idealistic children of the sixties, he figured he had finally grown up.

Kevin also recognized that Brandon's request was his awkward way of apologizing for misjudging Lacey, his way of making amends for years lost. Whether Brandon had made the gesture for himself or for Kevin's mother, Kevin felt he owed it to his father and to his own family to try to make it work. Lacey had been elated by the reconciliation, if not by the decision to join Halloran Industries.

Kevin had joined the company more than a decade ago and there had been no regrets on his part, not at first, anyway. He threw himself into the job the only way he knew how—heart and soul. Only now, with his marriage and his very life at stake, was he beginning to understand what Lacey had been saying all along, that the cost might have been too high.

When he'd awakened earlier to find Lacey standing beside his hospital bed, he'd been reminded of those early days. He'd seen the familiar tenderness and compassion in her eyes. He'd detected the faint trace of fear that had reminded him of the scared girl who'd stolen his heart when he'd been a mere boy.

He had wanted more than anything to tell her everything would be all right as he had so often in years past. But for the first time in his life, he wasn't so sure he could rectify things. He just knew he had to try, that the vows he'd taken nearly thirty years ago still meant something to him.

Kevin could only pray that they still meant something to Lacey, as well.

Chapter Four

Lacey heard the phone ringing through a bone-deep haze of exhaustion. The shrill sound brought her instantly awake.

Kevin! Something had happened to Kevin, she thought as she fumbled frantically for the phone, her heart hammering.

"Yes, hello," she said, her voice still scratchy with sleep.

"Lacey, it's Dana. I'm sorry if I woke you."

Lacey tried to shake off her grogginess. "It's okay, dear. I was just taking a nap. I didn't get much sleep at the hospital last night. Is there news? Is Kevin okay?"

"He's doing well," her daughter-in-law reassured her. "Jason called about an hour ago. He'd been in to see him earlier. He said Kevin looked a hundred percent better than he did when we left last night. What about you, though? Are you okay? Yesterday must have been—" she hesitated, then said "—well, it must have been difficult with things the way they've been between you and Kevin."

The last part was said in an uncertain rush, as if Dana wasn't sure she should even broach the subject of Lacey's relationship with her husband.

Hoping to avoid any further probing, Lacey deliberately injected a cheerful note in her voice. "Other than being tired, I'm just fine."

The reply was greeted with a skeptical silence. "Could we have lunch?" Dana asked finally. "I'll pick something up and bring it over, if you don't feel like going out."

"Maybe another time," Lacey said evasively. Dana had an uncanny knack for getting to the heart of things. Her directness was one of her charms, but Lacey wasn't sure she was ready to talk about what she was feeling—not until she understood it more clearly herself.

Before last night, it had been months since Lacey had seen Kevin. Then to see him in a hospital bed. It had been her worst nightmare come true. Anxiety, anger and love had each taken turns, leaving her thoroughly drained and confused. How could she feel so much for a man she didn't even think she knew anymore?

"Are you anxious to get back to the hospital?" Dana questioned.

Lacey might have grabbed at the excuse, if she hadn't known the implications. "No. Actually I hadn't planned to stop by until this evening."

"Then there's no reason for me not to come over," her daughter-in-law declared decisively. "I won't let you put me off. You need someone to talk to and it might as well be me. Who knows these Halloran men better than you and I do? I'll be there in an hour."

She hung up before Lacey could think of a single thing to say to keep her away. Besides, maybe Dana was right. She did need to sort things out, and Dana knew as much as anyone what these Halloran men were like once they started with their bulldozer tactics.

Brandon's warning, combined with Kevin's plea for another chance had taken their toll. Lacey was already dreading going back to the hospital, fearing that she would succumb to the combined pressure without giving the decision nearly enough thought. Maybe Dana could help her to stiffen her resolve.

A shower did its part to revive her. By the time the doorbell rang, she'd swept her hair back in a French braid and pulled on gray wool slacks and the cheerfully bright, blue sweater Dana had given her last Christmas.

At the door Dana shrugged out of her coat, then looked Lacey over from head to toe and nodded in satisfaction. "Everyone should have a mother-in-law who looks like you. You're a walking advertisement for my designs."

Lacey grinned. "You look pretty snappy yourself. How much longer do you figure you'll be able to wear that outfit?"

"About another hour, if I skip lunch," Dana complained as she headed for the kitchen with her armload of carryout food. "I couldn't get the waistband snapped as it is. Fortunately the sweater covers the gap. If I'm this bad with three months to go, what will I look like by the time I deliver? Jason will have to roll me to the hospital on one of those carts they use for moving heavy crates."

"Believe me, he'll be too excited to worry about how you look." She studied Dana's sweater, a bold swirl of hot pink on a neon green background. "A new design? Just looking at you cheers me up."

"That's the idea. It's for the mass market line. What do you think?"

"I think you're going to make a fortune for that designer who's added them to his collection and for Halloran Industries. Brandon must be ecstatic."

Dana rolled her eyes as she spread a selection of deli salads on the kitchen table. "Actually Brandon is more interested in the timetable for producing his great grandchild. I swear he would take Lemaze classes with me if Jason would let him. Jason has already had to stop him from checking the references of the instructors."

"That man needs to find a woman of his own. Maybe then he'd stop meddling in all our lives," Lacey said as she put plastic plates, mismatched stainless flatware and paper napkins on the table.

Dana's eyebrows rose a fraction. "Still roughing it?"

"It is a far cry from the Halloran china and silver, isn't it? You should have seen Kevin's expression when he saw it."

"He's been here, then?"

"Yes, when I first moved in. He left convinced that I'd lost my mind. Brandon agreed. Jason, also, probably, though he's too polite to say it to my face."

"Well, we know why Kevin would hate it. As for Brandon, he can't imagine anyone not being madly in love with his son or grandson. He also thinks the Halloran life-style is the primary selling point. I agree with you that he needs to find some woman and fall in love again. Better yet, he should have to fight to win her over. I told him exactly that just the other day."

"What did he say?"

"That a girl my age shouldn't be meddling in the love life of her elders. I don't think he saw the irony."

"He wouldn't," Lacey agreed. "Brandon thinks his interference is a God-given right as patriarch of the Halloran clan."

Dana's expression turned quizzical. "Do I detect a note of bitterness?"

"Bitterness, resignation, maybe a little frustration."

"He's been cross-examining you about the separation again, hasn't he?"

"Brandon, Jason, even Kevin from his hospital bed. None of them seem to get it, even after all this time."

"I do," Dana said with such quiet compassion that it brought tears to Lacey's eyes.

She blamed the rare display of emotion on stress and gave her daughter-in-law a watery, grateful smile. "I think maybe you do. I didn't leave out of spite. I don't hate Kevin."

"Quite the contrary would be my guess," Dana said. "It hurts, doesn't it? It hurts to see someone you love changing before your eyes and feeling totally helpless to stop it."

Not for the first time, Lacey was astounded by Dana's insightfulness. "For a young woman, you sound very wise."

Dana shrugged off the compliment. "I watched my mother fade and then die after my father walked out on us. Then I saw Sammy turn from a wonderful kid into a teenager destined for real trouble. No matter what I said or did, it never made a difference. In the end all I could do was love them, anyway. Thank God Jason came along when he did. He's the one who finally got through to Sammy.''

Lacey patted her hand. "I'm sorry I never knew your mother. She must have been something for you to turn out to be so special.''

Lacey caught the unexpected tears shimmering in Dana's eyes before she turned away. The rare show of emotion surprised Lacey. Her daughter-in-law always seemed so composed.

"Thanks for saying that,'' Dana murmured. "Sometimes I forget what she was like before she changed. It's good to be reminded that she wasn't always so defeated, that there was a time when she was terrific and fun to be around.''

Finally she faced Lacey again, the tearful, faraway look in her eyes gone. "You never met my mother and yet you have an instinctive understanding of her. At the same time, I wonder if you see the side of Kevin that I see at work.''

"Meaning?'' Lacey questioned cautiously.

"Did you know that he personally went to the hospital to visit the child of one of the Halloran workers, when the boy was diagnosed with leukemia?''

Startled, Lacey shook her head. It was something the old Kevin would have done in the blink of an eye, but now? She wouldn't have believed it, if she hadn't known that Dana would never make up such a story.

"It's true," Dana said. "Jason told me he also gave the woman time off with pay to be with her son. And he sent the whole family off to Disneyworld for Christmas because the boy had always wanted to meet Mickey Mouse."

"Kevin did that?" Lacey asked softly.

"He did. From what I've seen since I started working there, Kevin likes to make everyone believe that he's all business, that the only thing he cares about is the bottom line. I don't think there's a worker at Halloran Industries, though, who hasn't been touched by his kindness at one time or another." She smiled at Lacey. "I thought you should know. Maybe it will help to put things in perspective."

Lacey nodded. "Thank you for telling me. Kevin never did."

"He wouldn't. He takes it for granted that it's part of his job. That's what I admire so much about him. He doesn't think that being considerate, that caring deeply about his employees' welfare is unusual. It's just the way he is."

"Yes," Lacey said, more shaken than she could say by the reminder of a generosity of spirit she had thought was lost, "it is the way he is."

Was it possible that things weren't quite as hopeless as she had imagined?

Kevin thought he detected something new and oddly hesitant in Lacey's blue eyes when she came to visit him that evening. She regarded him as if she weren't quite sure what to make of him. Her assessing glance puzzled him.

"I like your hair like that," he began tentatively, wondering if it was past time to be wooing her with compliments, no matter how sincerely spoken. He yearned for the right to brush back the silken strands that had escaped the pulled-back style. "You look like a girl again. That sweater becomes you, too. It matches your eyes. One of Dana's designs, I'll bet."

A blush of pink rose in her cheeks as she nodded, making him regret how long it had been since he'd told her how beautiful she was. "It's true," he continued. "Sometimes I look at you and it's as if time had stood still."

She grinned at that. "What's gotten into you today? Is there a little Irish blarney in that IV?"

"They don't tell me what sort of concoctions they put in there. Maybe it's truth serum. I do know I've felt a powerful need to see you. I worried you might not come back."

"I told you I would."

"Are you here because I'm at death's door or because you want to be here?"

She regarded him impatiently. "You are *not* at death's door, so don't try playing on my sympathy. You're going to be just fine."

"If I rest," he reminded her.

"Exactly."

"Who's going to make me?"

"You're a grown man. No one should have to make you listen to reason."

"Maybe I've forgotten what it's like to rest. Maybe I need someone around to show me." He met her gaze and held it. "I need you, Lacey."

Her lips parted, but before she could speak, Brandon slipped into the room. Kevin managed a rueful grin. "Your timing's lousy, Dad."

Brandon looked from Kevin to Lacey and back again, then nodded in obvious satisfaction. "Interrupting your courting, am I? I'm sure you'll remember right where you left off. Just wanted to say goodbye before I go get some sleep. These old bones of mine can't take another night on that poor excuse of a sofa in the waiting room." He glanced at Lacey. "Remind me to order up some new furniture for this place."

"I'm sure they'll appreciate it," Lacey said, already edging toward the door. "Why don't I leave you two alone. I don't think Linc wants two of us in here at a time."

"Lacey," Kevin said, stopping her before she could flee, "I won't forget."

"Forget what?"

"I won't forget what we were talking about," he answered meaningfully.

She scurried out the door, reminding him of the only other time he could recall seeing her flustered—the day he'd asked her to marry him. She had wanted so desperately to say yes. He'd been able to read that much in her eyes. She'd tried to weigh that desire against the implications, from Brandon's wrath to the certain end of his future in the family business.

"Yes," she had said hesitantly, then before he could whoop for joy, "No. Oh, Kevin, I couldn't bear it if our being together ruined your relationship with your father."

"Dad will survive this little setback to his plans. He always does."

"But there's nothing more important than family."

"We'll have our own family. You and I. Our children. It'll be enough for me. Will it be enough for you?"

"All I've ever wanted in my life was to love you."

"Then that's our answer, isn't it?" Kevin had said with the naive faith only a twenty-year-old can have. "All I've ever wanted is to make you happy."

For so many years love had been enough. Only lately had he realized that sometimes marriage took more than love. It took patience and understanding and a willingness to struggle through the bad times. It took listening and sharing and compromise.

Kevin knew, then, what he had to do, what it would take to win Lacey back, to convince her that what they had now was just as strong as what they'd had back then.

When Jason came in later, Kevin asked him to make arrangements to open their house on Cape Cod. "Call the caretaker and have him stock the refrigerator and put in a supply of firewood. I'm going there when I get out."

Jason's expression was concerned. "Shouldn't you stay in town, closer to your doctor?"

"I need to get away. I can't bear the thought of going back to that huge house again. Your mother hates it. Did you know that?"

Jason looked startled. "She does?"

"Always has. I insisted on buying it after I went to work with your grandfather. I thought we needed to make a statement, live up to the corporate image, some such nonsense. She put up with it when you were growing up, but once you'd moved out, she started talking again about moving, getting something smaller."

Kevin took a deep breath as he made another decision. "I want you to put it on the market. Maybe then she'll see that I'm serious about wanting a reconciliation."

"Dad, are you sure? I thought you loved that house."

"I loved what I thought it represented. Turns out it's just a house, and a lonely one at that."

"Are you planning to stay on the Cape?"

"If I can convince your mother to stay there with me, I just may."

Jason grinned. "You always could twist her around your little finger."

Kevin shook his head ruefully. "No, son. You've got that backward. All it took was a smile and she could make me jump through hoops. Guess I'd forgotten that because in recent years I haven't given her much to smile about."

"Want to tell me what that means?"

He grinned at his son. "No."

Lacey would know and that was all that mattered.

The next morning Kevin waited impatiently for Lacey's visit. She didn't come. She wasn't there when he moved into a private room. Nor had she arrived by the time he got his pitiful excuse for a dinner.

When Jason arrived at seven-thirty, Kevin swallowed his pride and asked, "Have you seen your mother today?"

"No. Why? Hasn't she been here?"

Kevin shook his head. "You don't suppose she's sick?"

"I'll check on her on my way home."

"Go now."

"But I just got here."

"I'll feel better knowing that your mother is okay. Maybe the stress of the past few weeks caught up with her. That terrible flu is going around."

Jason threw up his hands. "Okay, I'll go, but I think you're worrying about nothing. Dana usually talks to her during the day. I'm sure if anything were wrong she would have let me know."

Kevin watched as Jason pulled his overcoat back on. "You'll call me?"

"I'll call you. Now stop worrying and eat your dinner."

Kevin glanced at the bland scoop of mashed potatoes and the colorless chunk of chicken. "This is not dinner. It's a form of torture dreamed up by Linc Westlake. I don't suppose you could sneak me some of Mrs. Willis's chicken and dumplings?" he inquired hopefully, thinking of Jason's housekeeper's delicious cooking.

Jason grinned at him. "I'll check with the doctor. If he says it's okay, I'm sure Mrs. Willis will be thrilled to make it for you. Get some rest, Dad. Don't tire yourself out with worrying. It won't help."

Jason had been gone less than twenty minutes when the door opened and Lacey walked through, her expression harried.

"Hi," she said cheerfully. "You're looking better."

"Where have you been?" Kevin asked, unable to control the edge in his voice.

Lacey regarded him sharply. "You sound angry."

"Worried," he corrected. "And if I sound worried, it's because I was. I expected you hours ago."

"*Expected?*" she echoed softly.

Kevin heard the warning note in her voice, but couldn't keep himself from adding, "If you couldn't get by, you should have let me know. I just sent Jason to check on you."

"Why on earth would you do that?"

"I told you. I was worried."

Kevin could see that Lacey was fighting her temper. She'd always been independent. No doubt she'd grown more so during their separation, when she'd been accountable to no one for her actions. She drew in a deep breath and pulled a chair close to the bed. He noticed she didn't take off her coat, as if to indicate to him that she wasn't here to stay.

"Kevin," she began in that patient tone he'd heard her use on Jason when he was five and misbehaving, "I'm sure you are bored to tears in here," she continued, "but I can't be here every minute. I have other obligations."

"One of those committees, I'm sure."

The sarcastic barb brought sparks into her eyes. "May I remind you that I am on those committees because you thought it would be the thing for the wife of a Halloran to do."

He winced. "Sorry. You're right. Is that where you were?"

"No. As it happens, I've gotten involved with something else."

Something or some*one*, he couldn't help wondering. Kevin felt an ache deep inside as he realized that this was probably just one of many things he didn't know about how Lacey spent her time.

"Tell me," he said. He saw her slowly relax at the genuine note of interest in his voice.

"Another time," she said. "For now, tell me how you're feeling. You must have had a good day, since Linc moved you out of intensive care and into a private room so quickly."

"The day's better now that you're here."

Kevin reached for her hand. After a hesitation so light that only a man deeply in love with his wife would notice, she slipped her hand into his. Contentment swelled inside him and he realized with Lacey here he could sleep at last.

Later he would never be sure if Lacey's gentle kiss was real or something he had dreamed.

Chapter Five

Over the next several days Lacey realized her feelings about Kevin's continued rapid recovery were oddly mixed. Day by day his strength returned. It was almost as if he applied the same obsessive attention to healing that he did to everything else. It was both astonishing and reassuring to see.

Though Lacey hated herself for even thinking it, she couldn't help wondering what would happen when he was well, when she no longer would have these hospital visits as an excuse for seeing him. The prospect of letting go for the second time daunted her. And yet there was no going back, not on the basis of a few quick promises, which were all too likely to be broken. She'd made up her mind about that.

Unfortunately, there was a troubling and unmistakable glint of determination in Kevin's eyes every time he looked at her. She'd often seen that expression right before he or Brandon scored some business coup. Kevin was scheming and it made her very nervous. Worse, she had the sense that Jason was conspiring with him. Together, the two men she loved most in the world were formidable opponents.

"Okay, enough is enough. What are the two of you up to?" she demanded when she found them with their heads together at the end of Kevin's first week in the hospital.

Jason looked from her to his father and back again. Guilt was written all over his face. "I'm out of here," he said hurriedly, backing toward the door.

Hands on hips, Lacey stepped into his path. "Not so fast."

He gave her a quick peck on the cheek. "Gotta go, Mom. Dana's waiting for me in the car."

"She can wait another ten seconds."

"Couldn't you just ask Dad, if you want to know something?" he suggested hopefully. "He's the one with all the answers."

She glanced at Kevin and saw the old familiar twinkle in his eyes. It made her heart tumble, just as it always had. That twinkle was downright dangerous.

Lacey recalled the first time she'd seen that glint of mischief in his eyes. He'd used some super glue to seal their fifth-grade teacher's desk drawer shut. That drawer had held their report cards. Kevin hadn't been anxious to take his home.

Now he was scowling with mock ferocity at Jason. "Traitor," he murmured, but there was a note of laughter in his voice.

"Bye, Mom. See you, Dad. Good luck."

Lacey approached the bed cautiously. "Now just why would you be in need of luck?"

"I'm a sick man," he said in a pathetically weak tone that was so obviously feigned, Lacey almost burst out laughing.

"I need luck, prayers, whatever it takes," he added for good measure.

"Nice try," she said.

Kevin managed to look genuinely dismayed. "You don't believe me?"

"I don't believe you," she concurred. "Try again."

"Have you seen Linc today?"

Her gaze narrowed as the first faint suspicion flickered in her mind. "What does Linc have to do with this?"

"He's agreed to let me out of here on Sunday."

"Kevin, that's wonderful!" she blurted out instinctively before she caught the glimmer of satisfaction in his eyes.

"What's the rest?" she asked slowly.

He folded his hands across his chest and inquired complacently, "What makes you think there's anything more?"

"Oh, please. I know you. If it were a simple matter of getting out of here on Sunday, you wouldn't look so smug."

"Smug? I was aiming for helpless."

"You couldn't look helpless if you tried. Come on, spill it. What's the rest?"

"There's a condition to my release."

Lacey got an uneasy feeling in the pit of her stomach, as suspicion replaced amusement. "What condition?"

"That I have someone around to look after me."

She ignored the return of the obvious gleam in his eyes and asked briskly, "Isn't our housekeeper there?"

At the quick shake of his head, she very nearly moaned. He'd never liked the stiff, unyielding woman, but he'd never been willing to fire her, either. "Kevin, you haven't fought with her, have you?"

"Actually, I had Jason send her off to visit her sister in Florida."

"Tell her to come back. I'm sure she'd cooperate under the circumstances."

"Afraid not."

"Why?"

"Well, the truth of the matter is that I fired her."

"You what?"

"I was never there, anyway," he said defensively. "So you see, I can't go home."

"Then you'll go to your father's. Mrs. Farnsworth would love the chance to fuss over you."

"I suppose that would work," he said. "But you know Dad. It wouldn't be long before he'd want to have business discussions over breakfast, lunch and dinner."

There was more than a little truth in that, Lacey conceded reluctantly. She knew now exactly where Kevin was headed, had known all along that some version of this game would come up sooner or later. Even so, she didn't have a ready, convincing alternative.

"Jason has room," she said desperately.

"What about Sammy?" he countered neatly.

Obviously he'd planned this as skillfully as a master chess player, Lacey thought, trying to muster up her fading resolve as he went on.

"I'll need peace and quiet," Kevin added for good measure. "You can't expect a kid that age to be on good behavior for days on end. Besides, Dana shouldn't have to take care of a sick father-in-law when she's trying to prepare for a baby."

"I think she'll have plenty of time to prepare after you're fully recuperated," Lacey retorted dryly.

She didn't have a strong argument where Sammy was concerned, however. Kevin was right to be worried about Dana's younger brother. He would probably try to engage Kevin in heated video games. With her husband's spirit of competitiveness, he'd land right back in the hospital.

"You could be right about Sammy, though," she admitted reluctantly. "Maybe Jason could loan you Mrs. Willis and you could just stay at home."

"I have a better idea," Kevin said cheerfully.

"Why doesn't that surprise me," she muttered darkly, envisioning the two of them in her cramped little apartment or, worse yet, back in their own home.

"I thought you and I could go to the Cape. It would be peaceful there this time of year."

Peaceful? she thought, stunned by the suggestion. The two of them alone on Cape Cod? No, that wouldn't be peaceful. It would be lunacy.

Cape Cod was where they'd made love for the very first time. Cape Cod was where he'd proposed to her. Cape Cod was where Jason had been conceived. Cape Cod was chock-full of memories. She had no intention of subjecting herself to that kind of torture.

"No," she said adamantly, "absolutely not."

"It would be good for us, Lacey. You have to admit that."

Lacey felt as if the walls of the room were closing in on her. It wasn't just the early memories. Later, nostalgic for all they had shared on Cape Cod, they had bought a house there. It was the one outrageously expensive indulgence that she had approved of totally.

They had made a pact that no business problems could ever follow them there. That house had become their refuge, a place for quiet talks, long walks and slow, sensuous sex. Kevin had kept his part of the bargain—until the day he'd stopped going because he no longer had time for the simple pleasure of a relaxing, intimate vacation.

Of all the suggestions he might have made, this was the most wickedly clever. The memories they shared there were among their most powerfully seductive.

She met his gaze and saw that he knew exactly what he was asking of her.

"Please, Lacey," he coaxed. "You did promise we would talk."

She was shaking her head before the words were out of his mouth. "I didn't promise to move back in with you. It won't work, Kevin."

"It will if we want it to. I'm ready to try. What about you?" He studied her closely, then added, "Or have you given up on our marriage?"

There was no mistaking the dare. Lacey cursed the tidy way Kevin had backed her into a corner. He knew how desperately she wanted to salvage what they'd once had. If she turned him down, she was as much as admitting that she'd given up hope.

Or that she was afraid.

She couldn't deny the fear that curled within her at the thought of what might happen if she gave in to his plan. If she accepted, if she went to the Cape and nothing had changed, she wasn't sure she could bear the pain of another separation and inevitably a divorce.

Now at least the worst days were behind her. She'd begun picking up the pieces of her life, creating a world in which Kevin was no longer the center. She liked the strength she'd discovered within herself.

But if that strength were real, if she'd truly gained her independence, wouldn't she be able to cope no matter what happened? She could practically hear him taunting her with that, though in reality he said nothing. Maybe it was simply her brain arguing with her heart.

All of the questions and none of the answers flashed through her mind in no more than an instant. Lacey studied Kevin's face and saw the uncertainty, the wistfulness in his eyes. It mirrored what she felt in her heart, the hope that had never died.

"I'll go," she said finally. She'd thought the risk of leaving Kevin had been dangerous enough. The risk of going back was a thousand times greater. She had to try, though. She would never forgive herself if she didn't.

"Thank you," he said simply. And she knew from the way time seemed to stand still as she met his gaze that her decision had been the right one, the only one.

No matter how much it might hurt later.

Kevin had the entire, endless night to think about Lacey's answer. He knew what it had taken for her to overcome her reluctance. The look in her eyes had spoken volumes about the struggle that raged inside her. He swore that he would do whatever it took to overcome her doubts. He viewed the coming days as a honeymoon of sorts, a chance to put their marriage on a new, more solid footing.

And he began making careful plans.

"I'll take care of everything," Brandon announced the following morning when he learned of their arrangement, which he clearly viewed as permanent. "Over the years I've learned a thing or two about patching things up after a spat."

"I'm sure you have," Kevin agreed, recalling the flurry of expensive gifts that would pour in whenever his father and mother argued.

His mother would point to a piece of jewelry and say, "This was for the time he stayed the whole night through at the factory and forgot to call. And these earrings were for that time he didn't tell me he'd invited guests for dinner and showed up with two of his most important customers."

Kevin grinned at the memories, but held up his hand. "Slow down, Dad. I think I'll handle this one my way. Besides, Jason's already called the caretaker. The house will be ready for us."

"What about flowers? Never was a woman who could resist a few bouquets of flowers."

"Like the five dozen roses you sent Mom, when you forgot your anniversary? Or the orchids that came when you missed her birthday?"

Brandon scowled at him. "Okay, so I had a lousy head for dates. Your mother loved those flowers just the same."

"Yes, she did," Kevin said softly, "because they came from you. Let me deal with Lacey my own way, Dad."

Brandon went on as if he hadn't heard a word Kevin was saying. "Maybe I ought to take a drive out there and check on things. You can't trust strangers to remember everything."

Kevin groaned as he envisioned his father standing in the doorway to welcome them. Lacey would no doubt turn tail and run. Although, on second thought, she might welcome a buffer between them. Either way, Kevin had no intention of letting Brandon meddle in this particular scenario.

"Forget it, Dad. For a man who spent years trying to keep us apart, you're suddenly awfully anxious for us to get back together."

Brandon didn't rise to the bait. "I'm not one bit afraid to admit I've made mistakes in my life. A few of them have been doozies. I know what I did back then to try to ruin what you two had was wrong. Lacey's a fine woman. You couldn't have done better."

"I know that. I'm glad you can see it now, too."

"You think this plan of yours is going to work?" he inquired, his brow furrowed. "Seems mighty chancy."

Kevin sighed. "It is a risk. If it doesn't work, I'll just have to come up with another idea. I'm not going to let her go without a fight, Dad. Not a second time. Come on. Let's go for a walk around the corridor. I'm going to need all my strength back if I'm going into battle tomorrow."

As they walked the length of the hospital hallway, Kevin saw the elevator doors slide open. He paused and watched, unwilling to admit how much he was hoping Lacey would be among those getting off. When she emerged behind a group of nurses, he spotted her at once, astonished at how youthful she looked with her honey-blond hair skimming her shoulders, her cheeks tinted pink from the March winds.

She started toward his room, then noticed him out of the corner of her eye. She turned his way, a smile spreading slowly across her face.

"I like the fancy new pajamas," she said, grinning at the outrageously expensive pair Brandon had brought him from a British collection made with Halloran fabrics.

Kevin would never have worn them if the only alternative hadn't been one of those indecent hospital gowns. In fact, as he thought back, the last pair of pajamas he'd owned had had bunny rabbits on them and he'd been going to sleep with a pacifier.

"What's wrong with them?" Brandon demanded. "This is one of the finest cottons we make. Do you have any idea what they charge for these things?"

"Settle down, Dad. I'm sure Lacey is truly awed by the quality."

"Awed isn't quite the word I had in mind," she teased. "I think I saw a pair just like these in some forties movie with Claudette Colbert. Or was it Katharine Hepburn?"

"Okay, enough, you two," Brandon grumbled. He shot a pointed glance at Kevin. "You could be walking up and down these hallways with your bottom bare."

Kevin sneaked a look at Lacey, whose lips were twitching as she fought the urge to laugh. She refused to meet his gaze. Brandon sniffed.

"Think I'll go off and leave you two alone. It's obvious you don't need me around anymore."

"Goodbye, Dad."

Lacey gave him a peck on the cheek and murmured something Kevin couldn't quite hear. From the amusement that immediately sparked in his father's eyes, Kevin had a hunch it had something to do with the damned pajamas.

When she finally turned back to Kevin, her expression was as innocent as a new baby's.

"What'd you say to him?" Kevin demanded.

"That's our secret."

"I thought secrets were taboo in a healthy marriage."

"Some secrets are taboo. Others add spice."

"You and my father have a secret that's going to add spice to our marriage?"

She grinned at him impishly. "You never know."

He regarded her indignantly. "You know, Lacey Halloran, it has occurred to me that locking myself away in a house on the Cape with you could drive me nuts."

"Not my fault," she claimed innocently. "It was your idea."

"And you intend to make me pay for that, don't you?"

"The regimen I have planned for you will make basic training seem like child's play."

He watched the play of light on her streaked blond hair and the sparks of mischief in her eyes. "What does Linc have to say about this plan you have?"

"Who do you think gave it to me?"

She waved several booklets without allowing him to catch a glimpse of the titles. He had to take her word for it when she flipped through them.

"'Cholesterol Management.' 'Triglycerides and You.' 'Exercise for the Healthy Heart.' 'The Low-Fat Diet.' And my favorite, 'Heart-Friendly Fruits and Vegetables.' I can hardly wait."

"I could still go to Jason's, you know. Sammy's beginning to look like a saint compared to my wife."

"I hear he has the newest video game. You very well might want to reconsider," she said agreeably.

He stopped where he was and framed her face with his hands. He could feel the heat climb in her cheeks. "Not a chance, Mrs. Halloran. Not a chance."

Chapter Six

The promise of long, quiet, intimate days on Cape Cod with Kevin terrified Lacey. It was possible—likely, even—that their expectations were entirely different. Anticipation and worry made the drive from the hospital to the Cape seem longer than ever.

What if Kevin only intended to lure her back, but hadn't thought beyond the challenge of the chase? she worried, when the first deadly silence fell.

She had little doubt that he could seduce her, that he could scramble her emotions and turn her best intentions to mush. Even in the worst of times, she had responded all too easily to his touch. The loving had been wonderful, but toward the end it hadn't been nearly enough. Now it would be a short-term solution at best.

A trip like this was what Lacey had been longing for, but now that Kevin had made the commitment to spend time with her, she wondered what would happen if they couldn't recapture what they had lost. In a last-ditch desperation, were they pinning too much on this time alone? Was she expecting something from Kevin that he couldn't possibly give?

As she clutched the steering wheel with white-knuckled intensity, her thoughts tumbled like bits of colored glass in a kaleidoscope, leaving her hopelessly confused.

Beside her, Kevin had settled back in the seat and closed his eyes, no more anxious to continue the struggle for nervous, meaningless small talk than she was.

With a bone-deep sorrow, Lacey couldn't help noticing the contrast to other trips they had made, times when the car had been filled with laughter and quiet conversation as they made the transition from their harried life-style in Boston to the relaxation of Cape Cod. Then even the silences had been lazy and comfortable. The anticipation had been sweet, not mixed with a vague sense of dread as it was now.

She breathed a sigh of relief when she finally pulled into the driveway of the rambling old house with its weathered gray shingles and white trim. A few hardy geraniums bloomed in the window boxes, the splashes of red against gray reminding her of an Andrew Wyeth painting she particularly loved.

She vividly recalled the precise moment when she and Kevin had first come upon this place, choosing it over all the others they had seen because of its haphazard wandering over a spectacular oceanfront piece of property. Later in the spring there would be daffodils and tulips everywhere and the scent of lilacs from a bush near the kitchen window.

Lacey glanced over and saw that Kevin was awake, his intense gaze closely examining the house that had once been so special to them.

"It looks neglected," he observed ruefully. "When was the last time we were out here?"

"Together?" she questioned pointedly. "Three years ago. We drove out for the day."

He regarded her with astonishment. "Surely that can't be."

"You've been too busy," she reminded him, trying—and failing—to keep the note of censure out of her voice.

He sighed. "That excuse must have worn thin. I remember how much you always loved coming here, especially this time of year before the summer crowds came back."

Kevin leaned closer, his breath fanning her face. He trailed his knuckles along her cheek, stirring her senses. She turned into the caress, and his fingers stroked her skin. The pad of his thumb skimmed provocatively over her lips.

"I'm sorry, Lace. I truly am."

She could tell from the look in his eyes that he really meant it, and something deep inside her shifted, making room for emotions she wasn't yet prepared to handle. Trying to ignore the trembly feeling he could still evoke in her, Lacey swallowed hard. She pulled away and summoned a smile.

"No more apologies, remember? We're here now." Her tone turned brisk. "We'd better get you inside. Linc wasn't all that thrilled that you wanted to come here, rather than stay in Boston."

"He just hates the fact that he won't be able to run up my bill with all those house calls," Kevin said as he opened the door and got out, following her to the trunk.

Instinctively he reached for a bag as they began the familiar ritual of unloading the car. Worried about the strain on his still-healing heart, Lacey quickly waved him off. "I'll get these."

A rare flash of anger rose in his eyes, then died just as quickly. "You're right," he said stiffly. "I'll go unlock the door. I should be able to manage that much at least."

Lacey cursed the fact that she'd reminded him that for now he wasn't as vital and healthy as he'd always been. Kevin had never been able to cope with so much as a cold, hating the slightest sign of weakness in a body he'd always tested to the limits. He looked so strong, with his powerful shoulders and well-sculpted legs, that she herself could almost forget that inside he was not yet healed.

Tennis, sailing and, years earlier, football—he had played them all with demanding intensity. How difficult it must be for him now to defer the simplest tasks to her. Still, Linc's instructions had been specific, and she intended to follow them to the letter.

There was no sign of Kevin as she made the half dozen trips to carry their luggage inside. He had vanished as soon as he'd opened the front door for her.

After an instant's hesitation, Lacey placed his bags in the master bedroom and her own in the guest room across the hall. The width of that hall was no more than three feet, but she saw it as symbolic of the ever-widening chasm between them in their marriage.

Worried that Kevin was still not inside—on such a chilly, blustery day—his first out of the hospital—she went in search of him.

She found him at last in back of the house, standing atop of a distant sand dune. Wearing only a thin jacket, a knit shirt and jeans, he had his hands in his pockets, his shoulders hunched against the wind. He was staring out to a white-capped sea that roared its strength as it crashed against the shore.

Guessing a little of what he must be feeling, Lacey walked to his side, hesitated, then tucked her arm through his.

"It certainly is setting up a fuss today, isn't it?" she observed.

At first she didn't think he would answer her, either out of some lingering resentment or because he was lost in his own thoughts. Finally he glanced at her, then back to the ocean and said, "I'd forgotten what that sound is like, how it fills up your head, driving out all petty annoyances."

"Like a symphony. Isn't that what you told me once?"

Kevin shook his head, clearly bemused by the words. "Was I ever that poetic?"

"I thought you were."

He turned and met her gaze then. Lacey thought for a moment she could see straight into his soul. Such sadness. It made her ache to think of him hurting so deeply. Yet her own sorrow was just as deep, just as heart-wrenching.

"Past tense," he noted wearily.

This time she lifted her fingers to caress his cheek. "Don't," she said softly. "Please don't. We have to make a pact to stop looking back. We have to look ahead."

"I'm not sure I dare."

Surprised by the genuine note of dismay in his voice, she asked, "Why?"

"What if there's only emptiness? Without you, that's all it would be, you know."

Hearing him say the words, hearing him admit how much she meant to him should have made her feel deliriously happy. But she was no longer that shy, innocent girl who'd given her heart so freely. Instead, knowing all she did, she felt this terrible pressure— pressure to forget the differences that had brought them to this moment, this place.

A part of Lacey wanted to give in now and promise him that everything would be as it always had been. She desperately needed to believe that coming here had been enough to reassure her. But the part of her that listened to her brain, rather than her heart, knew it was far too soon for either of them to make a commitment like that. Despite the pretty words, Kevin was no more ready for promises than she was.

She touched his cheek again, her splayed fingers warm against his chilled flesh, the gesture meant to comfort, not to promise. Their gazes met, caught, lingered. The silent communication was filled with hope and wistful yearning.

"I'm going to start dinner," she told him after several seconds passed. "Don't stay out here too long. It will be dark soon and the air is already cold and damp."

His gaze once again on the sea, he nodded and let her go.

Inside, Lacey found the refrigerator already well stocked with groceries, including a container of clam chowder left by the caretaker with a note saying it was from his grandmother. She poured it into a cast iron kettle on the stove, turned the flame on low and went to check more thoroughly on the rest of the house.

Everything had been readied for them. A fire had been laid and extra wood was stacked beside the hearth. Without the salty haze that would be back again within hours, the just-washed windows glistened with the last soft rays of sunlight. The wide plank floors had been rubbed to a soft glow, the furniture polished with something that smelled of lemons.

Best of all, a huge basket of her favorite spring flowers—daffodils, tulips and lily of the valley—added a cheerful finishing touch. Brandon's romantic idea, no doubt.

If Lacey hadn't known how long the house had stood empty, she might have believed she and Kevin had been here only yesterday. As it was, she hadn't been able to bear more than a quick day trip now and again. Alone, she had been all too vividly reminded of what she and Kevin had lost. The ache in her heart had been too much so she had never lingered.

Now she touched the automatic lighter to the kindling in the fireplace. Within minutes the flames had caught and a cozy warmth stole through the chilly room.

Back in the kitchen she grabbed a handful of silver and a pair of placemats and set places on the coffee table in front of the fire. When they were here alone, they rarely ate in the formal dining room or even in the huge old kitchen, preferring the intimacy of meals in front of the fire's warmth. Only on the hottest days of summer did the routine vary and then they moved to the beach, where they could listen to the waves and watch the stars as they ate by candlelight.

Kevin came in just as she was pulling a loaf of crusty, homemade bread from the oven. His eyes lit up as he shrugged out of his jacket and tossed it over the back of a chair.

"Is that what I think it is?" he asked, coming closer to sniff the wonderful aroma.

"Mrs. Renfield's homemade bread," she confirmed. "And her New England clam chowder. Your favorites."

"What can I do to help?"

"If you'll take the bread in, I'll bring the soup. That should do it."

"I don't suppose she left one of her peach pies in the refrigerator."

"Sorry," Lacey said, amused at his immediately disappointed expression. "Looks like a cherry cobbler to me. And don't tell me you didn't know perfectly well that she was going to leave all this for you. You probably called her up and pleaded with her."

"I did no such thing."

"Then you had Jason do it."

He grinned at her. "Okay, maybe I did suggest he drop a few hints."

"Are you sure he didn't do more than that?"

"Such as?"

"Sending her a few bolts of that outrageously expensive fabric she loves so much."

Kevin grinned guiltily. "A few yards, not a few bolts."

"Do you realize that that seventy-five-year-old grandmother uses that cloth to whip up fancy pot holders for the church bazaar?"

"She does not," he said, his expression clearly scandalized at the waste.

Lacey picked up one of the pot holders she'd used to carry in the steaming bowls of chowder. "Recognize this?"

Kevin groaned. "Oh, dear Lord. Don't ever let Dad see that."

"Too late. He bought up every one she had at the bazaar last year. He was terrified one of Halloran's customers would see them and realize they were designing ball gowns made out of the same material."

Lacey felt her lips curving into a smile as Kevin's laughter bubbled forth. It had been so long since she'd heard him sound genuinely happy.

"Can you imagine Miriam Grayson discovering that her latest couture creation matched Mrs. Renfield's pot holders?" Kevin said, still chuckling. "Her designer would wind up skewered with one of her lethal, pearl-tipped hat pins."

"I believe Brandon mentioned the same scenario. For about thirty seconds he actually seemed tempted to risk it."

"I'm not surprised. Old Miriam is a pompous pain in the you-know-what. However, her designer is one of Halloran's best customers. Dad obviously had second thoughts the minute he envisioned the impact on the company's bottom line."

As silly and inconsequential as the conversation was, Lacey couldn't help thinking it was the first time in months that she and Kevin had actually shared so much carefree laughter. She would have to remember to thank Mrs. Renfield by slipping her a few yards of that emerald-green silk that would go so well with her bright eyes—after warning her to use it on a dress, not pot holders.

The tone of the evening seemed set after that. Kevin and Lacey reminisced about other trips and other neighbors. They recalled clam bakes and bake sales, art festivals and favorite restaurants. Here, unlike Boston, they had always felt part of the quiet, casual rhythm of the community, had had time for neighborly visits and lingering over tea.

Lacey felt Kevin's gaze on her and regarded him quizzically. "What?"

"This is the way I always think of you," he said, brushing a strand of her hair back and letting it spill through his fingers.

"How?" she said. Her breath caught in her throat as her pulse scrambled wildly.

"The firelight in your hair, your eyes sparkling, a smile on your lips. Are you happy to be here, Lacey?"

Unable to speak, she simply nodded.

"With me?"

That question was more difficult to answer honestly. Being here with Kevin was bittersweet at best. She could almost believe things were perfect. Almost.

And then she would remember.

He sighed. "Obviously, I shouldn't have pressed," he said, his voice tight.

Stricken by the hurt in his eyes, she said, "Kevin, this isn't a quick fix. It's a beginning."

He nodded, then stood up. "I'm more tired than I thought."

Lacey started to force him to stay, force him to confront the very real ordeal ahead of them. Then she bowed to the exhaustion on his face. "Your things are in the master bedroom."

"And yours?" he asked very slowly.

"Across the hall. I thought it was best."

"As always, I'm sure you're right," he retorted not attempting to conceal the sarcasm. He pivoted then and walked away, leaving Lacey alone to face the fire and the long, empty hours ahead before sleep would claim her.

Kevin stood at the window of the master bedroom, his eyes gazing blankly into the darkness of a moonless night. The sound of the waves did nothing to soothe him.

Maybe this had been a terrible idea, after all. Maybe instead of bringing him and Lacey closer, staying here would only remind her of what had gone wrong.

What did she want? he wondered angrily. Lacey had always expected him to live up to some impossible ideal, and he'd tried. Lord, how he had tried. But in the end, he'd proven himself to be a mere mortal. Maybe that would never be enough for her.

He listened as the door across the hall closed softly, and he found his hands balling into fists.

Rest, Linc had told him. How could he rest, when the woman he loved was holding him at a distance, when his body ached to feel her next to him again?

He hadn't grown used to the emptiness of their huge bed in Boston. Though this one was smaller, it would be just as cold and unwelcoming without her there beside him. He stared at it bleakly, and for one brief second he considered grabbing his blankets and sleeping in one of the other guest rooms.

Kevin saw the folly of that at once. He could sleep in any bed in the house and Lacey's nearness would taunt him. He would sense her presence in his very gut. The unmistakable, seductive scent of her favorite floral perfume was everywhere in this house. He would lie there surrounded by her, yet unable to touch her.

Exhaustion finally propelled him across the room. He stretched out on the bed, the sheet skimming his naked flesh and reminding him all too clearly of his wife's first, delicate caresses. The aching arousal was almost painful, but in its own way reassuring. If the attraction burned this brightly for him, surely it could not have died for Lacey. It would take time, that was all. Time to discover each other anew. Time to heal.

Time to fall in love all over again.

Chapter Seven

If they had ended the previous evening walking on eggshells, the morning was starting out to be a hundred times worse. Lacey was so painfully careful and polite Kevin was sure he was going to scream.

Not that he could blame her after the way he'd treated her when he'd found out about the sleeping arrangements. Morning had given him a different perspective on how he'd handled things. Had he honestly expected her to tumble into his arms just because she'd agreed to come to the Cape with him? Hoped, maybe. Expected, no.

As he'd anticipated, their bed had seemed incredibly empty without her. He'd lain awake for hours wishing she were close enough to touch, wishing he could feel the soft feathering of her breath against his skin. He'd ached for just a hint of their old physical intimacy. Toward dawn he had reconciled himself to the unlikelihood of that happening for weeks, maybe longer. Not until she trusted him again.

Even though Kevin accepted much of the blame for the way things were between them, the saccharine politeness to which Lacey was now subjecting him grated.

"More decaf?" she inquired, every bit as solicitous as a well-trained waitress, and just as impersonal.

"No," he responded curtly. He blamed the surliness in his tone on the hours he'd spent counting sheep and trying not to think of Lacey in that bed across the hall.

"Another piece of toast?"

"I've had plenty."

"Did you want the A section of the paper?"

"No."

"Sports?"

"No."

Lacey nodded and retreated behind the local section. In self-defense Kevin grabbed the section atop the stack in front of her. Business, he noted with a modicum of enthusiasm. Maybe that would keep his mind occupied. He could concentrate on mergers and takeovers, instead of the way Lacey's ice-blue sweater clung to her curves and brought out the color of her eyes.

One of the hazards of being in the textile business, he'd discovered long ago, was the need to scrutinize fabrics. When they were worn by his wife, it was doubly difficult to focus his attention elsewhere.

Damn, he hated the last instruction Linc had given him. No sex, the doctor had warned. At Kevin's horrified expression, he'd added, "Soon, but absolutely not right away. A little patience won't hurt you."

That was easy for Linc to say. He wasn't seated across the table from a woman he hadn't held in his arms for months, a woman who had never seemed so desirable or so aloof. Kevin knew that if he could just hold Lacey, caress her, then the distance and uneasiness between them would melt away.

Instead, he was going to have to rely on his wits. The prospect daunted him. Maybe if he thought of this as a deal he needed to close, a strategy would come to him. The thought of Lacey's reaction to being compared with a business deal brought a smile to his lips.

She folded the last section of the paper and apparently caught him still grinning.

"What's so funny?"

"Nothing," he said hurriedly. "What would you like to do today?"

"Do?" she repeated blankly. "You're here to recuperate, not to fill up every spare minute. It's called relaxation. You do remember how that works, don't you?''

''Barely,'' he admitted.

She nodded and he could see from the amusement in her eyes that the dark mood had lifted. He wasn't deceiving himself, though. It could return as quickly as it had gone.

''Then lesson one is that we make no plans,'' Lacey said. ''We do whatever we feel like doing. For starters, there's a stack of new books in the living room. And since it looks as if it's going to pour any minute, that makes this the perfect day to curl up in front of the fire with a good book.''

''Sounds good to me. Did you bring that new management book? I haven't had time to get to it yet.''

Lacey shot him a disapproving frown. ''No management books. Try mysteries, political thrillers, maybe a biography, as long as it's not about some titan of industry. Remember when we used to spend all day sitting out back, doing nothing more than reading and sipping iced tea?''

''Vaguely. Are you sure I wasn't reading management books?''

She grinned. ''Positive.''

''Political tracts?''

''Afraid not.''

''I was reading fiction?'' He was incredulous.

She nodded. "At the beach you read fiction. Actually I take that back. If I recall correctly, you fell asleep with the books in your hands. I can't swear that you read any of them."

"No wonder not one single plot comes back to me."

She smiled, then, and leaned closer. To his surprise she laced her fingers through his.

"It's going to be okay," she promised. "This awkwardness will pass."

"Will it?" he questioned doubtfully. "Sometimes I feel as if I'm an amnesiac trying to recall a part of my life that's completely blanked out. You seem to have such a vivid recollection of the way things used to be."

Lacey sighed and withdrew her hand. "Maybe I do live too much in the past. Maybe it's wrong to want to go back. But I think about how perfectly attuned we were, how much we treasured quiet moments, and I can't help having regrets. Now we can't even get through a single evening without arguing."

Kevin couldn't deny the truth in that. "We aren't the same people we were when we met. Lacey, we were eleven years old. We were kids."

"We were the same way when we were twenty-one, even thirty-one," she reminded him, suddenly angry. "We were on the same wavelength. We shared everything. We could practically finish each other's sentences, though thank God we didn't. It all started to change—"

"When I went to work at Halloran," he finished for her, his own temper flaring. How long did she intend to throw that decision back in his face? "Why is going to work for my father so terrible? Jason's there, too. I don't hear you criticizing him for making that choice."

"It was his *choice,* Kevin. It was what he always wanted. You were railroaded into it by Brandon."

The last of Kevin's patience snapped. "Was our life so rosy before that? Don't you remember the way we had to squeeze every last penny out of every dollar we made? Don't you remember the nights I came home so frustrated and angry that my jaws ached from clenching my teeth? Don't you remember how we both woke up one day to the fact that no matter what we did, no matter how hard we worked to fight the system, the system wasn't going to change unless we worked within it?" He slammed his fist down on the table. "For God's sake, Lacey, we aren't idealistic children anymore."

Her eyes widened during his tirade, then slowly filled with hurt. "Is that what you think, that I haven't grown up? Is that it, Kevin? If so, then maybe we're wasting our time here, after all."

Her jaw set, she picked up the breakfast dishes and carried them to the counter. Her back to him, he could see the deep sigh shudder through her in the instant before she slammed the dishes down so hard it was a wonder they didn't shatter. She grabbed her jacket from a peg by the back door and stormed out, leaving him filled with rage and the uneasy sense that this brief but cutting argument might well have been their last.

He hadn't meant to accuse her of immaturity. It wasn't that at all. But it was true that she tended to cling to ideals, rather than deal with the practicalities. Looking at Halloran's bottom line had put things into the right perspective for him. He'd been able to provide for his family, give them the way of life they deserved. He had helped Brandon to make the company even stronger, kept him from at least some of his own wild schemes that would have cut deeply into their profits. Jason would have a legacy now, as would his child. What more did Lacey want from him?

Kevin waited anxiously after that, starting each time he thought he heard a sound. He wanted to finish the argument, make her see his point of view for once.

His frayed nerves grew worse with each passing hour. By mid-morning, with rain pelting the windows with the force of sleet, he was worried sick. Where was she?

He consoled himself with the thought that no one would stay outdoors in weather like this. Surely she had taken refuge with one of the neighbors. He glanced repeatedly out the front window to reassure himself that the car was still in the driveway, that she'd hadn't taken it and fled.

When Lacey wasn't back by noon, worry turned to anger. She had to know what she was doing to him, he thought. She could have called, let him know that she was safe and dry.

As quickly as the fury rose, though, it abated. What if she weren't safe? What if she had fallen and hurt herself? What if she were cold and wet, stranded on the beach somewhere, caught by a rising tide? *What ifs* chased through his mind and turned the canned soup he'd forced himself to eat into acid in his stomach.

It was nearly one o'clock when Kevin heard Lacey's footsteps on the back porch. He threw open the door and found her standing there looking soaked and bedraggled. Even as he met her gaze, he saw her shiver, her whole body trembling violently. The patches of color in her cheeks were too vivid. Her lips had an unhealthy bluish tint. She looked as if she might keel over into his arms.

"My God," he murmured, pulling her inside. "Did you decide to go for a swim?"

Her teeth chattered as she tried to answer.

Fury evaporated as he focused on her needs. There would be time enough for recriminations later. "Never mind," he said. "Let's get you out of these clothes and into a warm tub."

He reached for her jacket, but she pushed his hands away. "To-o-o c-c-old," she murmured.

"Well, this soggy mess won't do much to change that. Come on, Lacey, take it off. I'll go get you a blanket and you can sit in front of the fire while I run the bath water."

Teeth still chattering, she nodded finally and began working at the buttons. Satisfied that she was going to follow instructions, Kevin went into the bedroom and pulled the quilt off his bed. When he got back to the kitchen with it, he halted in the doorway, his expression stunned.

Lacey had stripped down to her underwear—scraps of lace that hid nothing, including the fact that her nipples had peaked into hard buds from the chill air. He drew in a ragged breath and forced himself to sacrifice his need to study every inch of her lovely, fragile body that had changed so little through the years. He wrapped her in the quilt and held her close until the violent shivering stopped.

With his chin resting on the quilt draped over her shoulders, he asked, "Better?"

"Much," she said, her voice finally steady.

"Then go sit in front of the fire, okay?"

Lacey nodded, then turned to meet his gaze. "Thanks."

"For what?"

"For not telling me what a fool I am."

He grinned. "I'm saving that for later."

After an instant's pause she managed a wobbly grin of her own. "I should have known."

When the bath water had been drawn and the tub was filled with her favorite fragrant bubbles, he called her into the bathroom. She drew in a deep breath of the steamy air.

"Heaven," she declared.

"I'll warm up some soup for you. Don't stay too long," he said, wishing he dared to linger, wishing she would invite him to join her in that oversized tub as she had so often in the past. Imagining her skin slick and sensitized beneath his touch made his body grow taut.

Her gaze rose to meet his, and he could tell from the smoldering look in her eyes that she remembered, too, and that she could see exactly what the memories were doing to him. "I won't be long," she promised.

Reluctantly Kevin closed the door, then leaned against it, suddenly weak with longing. Oh, how he ached for her. How badly he wanted to hold her, to caress her, to claim her once more as his own. The longing spread through him, a slow flame that warmed and lured. If he knew anything at all about his wife, she too was burning. She too was filled with a sweet, aching need that nothing short of tender caresses and uninhibited passion would satisfy.

He forced himself to go back into the kitchen, to throw Lacey's soggy clothes into the washer, to pour a healthy serving of soup into the saucepan on the stove. The routine got him through the worst of the wanting. He was even able to have a perfectly rational discussion with himself about the dangers of rushing things.

Not that it meant a hill of beans when Lacey walked back into the kitchen with her blond hair curling damply around her face, her skin glowing from the fragrant steam. His body told him exactly what he could do with all of his rationalizations.

The only thing that saved him from making an absolute fool of himself was the way his wife pounced on the soup as if she hadn't eaten in days. Only when she'd finished the entire bowl, sighed and leaned back to sip a cup of tea did he dare to speak.

"Where did you go this morning?" He was proud of the casual tone.

"For a walk on the beach."

"In the pouring rain? Were you that furious with me?"

She shrugged. "I was furious, but the truth of the matter is that it wasn't raining when I left. I was a couple of miles up the beach before it got really bad. I started to head back, but by then the tide had come in and I couldn't get around the point. When I realized it wasn't going to let up anytime soon, I climbed the cliff."

Kevin's eyes widened. "You're terrified of heights."

"I'm not so thrilled with the idea of catching pneumonia, either. I figured climbing was the lesser of two evils. I only panicked once when I made the mistake of looking down. It wasn't all that far, but it looked damned treacherous and slippery."

"It *is* treacherous and slippery. You could have broken your neck."

"But I didn't," she said, looking pleased with herself.

He hesitated, then finally said, "Should we talk about what happened this morning?"

Her smile faded. "Not now. I'm exhausted."

Though he was reluctant to put the discussion off any longer, he nodded. "Go on and take a nap then. I'll clean up here."

She shook her head. "I think I'll go sit in front of the fire instead."

She stood up and started for the door, then turned back. "Kevin?"

He stopped halfway between the table and the sink. "Yes?"

"Will you come join me when you're finished?"

Irritated that even this small overture aroused him to a state of aching desire, he nearly refused. Then he caught the wistfulness in her eyes and realized that to deny them both a moment's pleasure was absurd.

"I'll be there in a minute," he promised.

* * *

Lacey wasn't entirely sure what impulse had made her ask Kevin to join her in the living room. Goodness knew the man had infuriated her earlier with the suggestion that she was behaving immaturely just because she wanted her husband healthy and happy again. Of course, she'd only added proof to his claim by running out. She should have stayed and talked, held her temper and listened to his explanation. That was the only way this was going to work.

They needed so desperately to talk. She needed to comprehend why he'd been so quick to condemn her attitude. He needed to understand exactly what she was trying to recapture. They both needed to discover if there was any common ground left at all. They couldn't do that without putting all their cards on the table, even the ones most likely to hurt.

She was too tired now to get into it again, but asking Kevin to join her in the living room had been an overture, at least. It had been impossible to miss the longing in his eyes when he'd come upon her in the middle of the kitchen with nothing but bra and panties keeping her decent. That longing had turned to desire as he'd stood beside the tub watching her lower herself into the foam of lilac-scented bubbles. Lacey knew exactly what Kevin was feeling, because it had taken every ounce of willpower she possessed to refrain from inviting him to share the bath with her.

All the talking and listening would have to wait, though. Now she wanted nothing more than to curl up on the sofa and stare at the mesmerizing flames. She wanted only to let the fire's heat soak into her bones.

As it did, she could feel herself relaxing, feel her eyes drifting shut. She blinked and forced herself awake. She wanted to stay awake until Kevin was by her side, but tension, exercise and fear had exhausted her. Her eyes closed again.

She had only the vaguest sense when Kevin joined her on the sofa. When he whispered her name, she thought she responded, but couldn't be sure. Then she felt herself being resettled in his arms, and it was as if she'd come home at last. A sigh trembled on her lips, and then she slept as she hadn't slept in all the lonely months they'd been apart.

Chapter Eight

Kevin stood in the doorway of the kitchen watching the play of sunlight on Lacey's hair. She'd left it loose, not bothering to tame the haphazard curls that framed her face. It shimmered with silver and gold highlights, reminding him of the way it had looked on their wedding day.

There was something radiant and serene about her today, just as there had been then. However she felt about yesterday's disagreements, she had obviously pushed them out of her mind. She looked beautiful, despite the fact that she was elbow-deep in dirt that was still damp from the previous day's rain.

"What on earth are you doing?" he inquired as she scowled fiercely at something she saw.

In response, a clump of weeds flew over her shoulder and landed at his feet.

"I'm trying to make some order out of this mess. The weeds have taken over," she muttered without turning to look at him.

"Why don't you call Rick Renfield and have him do it? Isn't that what we pay him for?"

"We pay him to keep an eye on the house, to make sure the pipes don't freeze, to see that the grass is cut. I doubt he knows the first thing about gardening."

"And you do?"

Lacey turned, then, and swiped a strand of hair out of her face with the back of her wrist. The impatient gesture left a beguiling streak of dirt across her cheek. The curly wisp promptly blew forward again.

Unable to resist, Kevin walked closer and knelt down. His fingers brushed the silken strand back, then lingered against her sun-kissed skin. With the pad of his thumb, he wiped away the smudge of dirt. He could almost swear he felt her tremble at the innocent caress.

She gazed up at him and his heart stilled.

"You've forgotten that I was the one who put in all the flower beds at our first house," she said. "I landscaped that entire yard."

He regarded her with a faint sense of puzzlement. "I thought you just did that because we didn't have the money back then to hire somebody."

"I did it because I enjoyed it," she said almost angrily, backing away from his touch. "When we moved, you hired a gardener and I never had the chance again. Tomas wouldn't even let me near the rose bushes to clip them for the house, much less indulge me by letting me plant something."

"Why didn't you say something?"

"To him?"

"No. To me."

"I did," she said. "You never listened."

He heard the weary resignation in her tone and winced. "I'm sorry. I guess I thought you'd prefer to spend your time on all those committees you were forever joining."

"And you were wrong," she said curtly. "I joined those committees because you wanted me to and because there was nothing left for me to do at home. We had a gardener and a housekeeper. If Jason had been younger, you probably would have insisted on a nanny."

Kevin stood up and shoved his hands into his pockets. "Most women would kill to have full-time household help, especially with a house as large as ours and with all the entertaining we needed to do."

"I am *not* most women."

For emphasis she jammed a trowel into the rain-softened earth and muttered something more, something he couldn't quite make out. He decided it was just as well. He doubted it was complimentary.

Again Kevin wished that their first tentative steps toward a reconciliation weren't so incredibly awkward. So many things seemed to be blurted out in anger, complaints long buried. Once minor, now they seemed almost insurmountable.

He wondered if Lacey was right. Had she told him all this before? Had he failed to listen, sure that he was giving her what she wanted, rather than what he thought she deserved?

There were times he felt as if he were learning about this woman all over again, rather than simply picking up the threads of a relationship that had weathered more than a quarter of a century. He tried to accept that it was going to take time, that two people who had apparently lost the ability to communicate what was in their hearts weren't going to relearn the skill overnight.

"I was thinking of going for a walk on the beach," Kevin said finally, unwilling to pursue the dangerous direction of their conversation on such a beautiful afternoon. They needed time just to be together, not a nonstop confrontation.

"It's a beautiful day for it," Lacey said, then added sternly, "Remember not to overdo it. Even though you've made remarkable progress, Linc wants you to take it easy.''

That said, she seemed to be waiting, but for what, he wondered. An invitation? Surely she knew she was welcome. Then again, nothing could be taken for granted as it once had been. "Want to come along?" he asked.

For an instant he thought she was going to refuse, using the gardening as an excuse. He could see the refusal forming on her lips when she turned her face up to meet his gaze, then something shifted. Her mouth curved into a faint smile.

"Sure," she said, taking off her gardening gloves and tossing them aside. "Let me get a sweater. The wind is probably colder down by the water."

Kevin nodded and watched her go inside. When she emerged, a bulky red sweater topped her snug-fitting jeans. He had a hunch it was one of his daughter-in-law's designs. It was certainly far bolder than what Lacey usually wore in town. There she tended to stick to cashmere and pearls, as understated and elegant as any society matron in the city.

In fact, with his hours at work and his business commitments, he had seen her more often in sleek designer evening wear than anything casual. With her quiet grace, her stunning figure and youthful complexion, she had done the name of Halloran proud, after all. Even Brandon had admitted that.

Kevin thought it was odd that he was only now realizing that he liked her better this way. It reminded him of the girl he'd fallen in love with, the girl in hand-me-downs who'd felt the needs of others so deeply, the girl who'd learned to overcome her shyness in order to fight for the things in which she believed with all her heart.

Including their marriage.

As much as it troubled and angered him, Kevin knew that's what Lacey had been doing when she'd walked out the door of their Boston home months ago. She hadn't left in defeat or even fury. She had left with the hope that her daring ultimatum would get his attention as nothing else had.

If it hadn't been for this most recent heart attack, he wondered if they would be here today or whether his stubborn refusal to acknowledge the validity of her claims would still be keeping them apart.

Knowing that somehow he had to fight for each precious moment until he could regain her trust, he held out his hand. After an instant's hesitation, she took it. They climbed over the dunes to reach the hard-packed sand by the water's edge.

The ocean was quieter today, its pace late-afternoon lazy as it shimmered silver gray in the sun. He felt good holding his wife's hand again as the sun's warmth kissed their shoulders and a cool breeze fanned their faces.

"Remember," he began at the same time she did. He glanced into her eyes and saw the laughter lurking in the blue depths. "You first."

"I was just remembering the first time we came here."

"To this house or to the Cape?"

"To this house. Your hand shook the whole time you were writing out the check for the deposit. I think in the back of your mind you viewed it as selling out to the establishment. You spent the whole weekend looking as if you expected the activist brigade to catch you and make you turn in your young idealist credentials. I was terrified you were going to back out."

"I still get a pang every now and then," he admitted candidly. "Especially when I think of how many people are homeless."

"Which explains why, the very next week, you donated money to create a homeless shelter. For a few anxious days I was afraid you were going to try to donate this place."

"Back then if it hadn't been for the zoning problems, I probably would have."

"And now?"

"I'm grateful you talked me into it. It's the one place where I feel as if we connect."

Lacey nodded. "I feel that, too. It's because it's the one place where we have only happy memories. We never allowed our differences to follow us here."

Kevin returned her gaze evenly, pained by the depth of hurt that shadowed her blue eyes.

"And when the differences got to be too much to put aside, I just stopped coming," he admitted, certain that she would be angered or at the very least hurt by the brutal honesty. To his surprise she was nodding as if it were something she'd realized long ago.

"I know," she confirmed softly. "That made me saddest of all. We've lost three years here, years we can never get back. We missed the flowers blooming in the spring, the lazy summer days, the change of the leaves in the fall. Even before we were married, Cape Cod was where we always came to witness the changing of the seasons. Now the seasons just rush by."

"Don't," he whispered, pausing by the edge of the water and cupping her chin. "Don't count them as lost. We can learn from them. We can build on a foundation that's all the stronger for having weathered this crisis."

As tears welled in Lacey's eyes, Kevin drew her slowly into his arms, holding her loosely. At first she was stiff, but in no more than a heartbeat she began to relax, her arms circling his waist, her head resting against his chest, where he was sure she could hear his heart thunder.

The scents of salt water and flowery perfume swirled around him as he gave himself over to the sensations that just holding her stirred. His blood roared in his veins, then slowed as contentment stole over him. When had he last felt this peaceful? Months ago? Years?

"When you say it like that," she murmured, the words muffled against his chest, "I can almost believe we will work things out."

"Believe it, Lacey. I want it with all my heart."

"So do I."

But they both knew that wanting alone was not nearly enough.

Lacey was standing in front of the kitchen counter up to her elbows in bread dough and flour. She studied the mess and wondered what had possessed her to try to bake bread, when the best bakery in the universe was less than a mile away, to say nothing of Mrs. Renfield, who would gladly trade one of her home-baked loaves for more of that fancy material.

Maybe it had something to do with the confession she'd made the day before. It was true that she had resented giving up the claim to her own kitchen, her own gardens. She had spoken out, but obviously not forcefully enough if Kevin had no memory of it. Maybe she had just given up, once it was clear that he'd made up his mind. Maybe it was her own fault, as much as his. For all of his talents, he wasn't a mind reader. If she had capitulated, he must have thought it was simply because he'd convinced her.

Maybe she was baking bread because she was still shaken by the way she had felt with Kevin's arms around her. Each time he touched her, each time he gazed into her eyes, each time she felt his kindness surrounding her like the warmth of a quilt, he stripped away some of her defenses. After that, Lacey had desperately needed a project that would give her time to re-group. What better way to do that than tackling something she'd never tried before?

Just as she was resolving never to give in so easily again to his persuasive arguments or his touches, she heard Kevin's muffled chuckle behind her and whirled on him. She shook a warning finger at him, sending out a fine mist of flour.

"Don't say it. Don't even think it."

His eyes sparkled with amusement. "I was just admiring your domesticity. I suppose this is one of those other things I robbed you of by hiring a housekeeper."

She heard the note of good-natured teasing in his tone, but she was in no mood for it, not with this mess spread out around her. "Do you recall my ever baking bread?"

"Nope."

"That's right. I never once attempted it, even before you hired the housekeeper. Thank goodness you never wanted to live in one of those communes where everyone baked their own bread and lived off the vegetables they grew themselves."

"Without toxic pesticides, of course."

She grinned. "Of course."

"So why are you baking bread now?"

"Because I should have learned," she said, aware as she said it how ridiculous she sounded.

"Excuse me?" Kevin queried, justifiably confused by her convoluted logic.

"I know how you like home-baked bread. It was something I always meant to learn, but first one thing and then another came along and I never did."

"So you're learning now?"

She swiped her hand across her face. "More or less. I stopped by Mrs. Renfield's while you were resting this afternoon and asked her for the recipe."

"Maybe you should have asked her for another loaf of bread."

Lacey scowled at Kevin for echoing her own thoughts. "Go away."

He nodded agreeably. "No problem. When should I come back?"

"Try breakfast. I figure I ought to have some semblance of bread figured out by then."

"We haven't had dinner yet."

"Don't you think I know that? I forgot about all that rising and kneading and stuff. It takes time."

"I'd really like some dinner." At her fierce expression, he quickly amended, "Not right away, but soon. Say, by eight?"

"So order a pizza," she growled.

His eyes lit up. "A pizza! Great idea." He reached for the phone.

"Wait!"

He turned back. "I knew it was too good to be true. No pizza, huh?"

"Chinese. Call for Chinese. Nothing fried, nothing with eggs. That should be healthy enough. I think there's a menu from a carryout place by the phone in the living room."

He then left her alone to pummel the damn dough and rue the precise moment when she'd had this brainstorm. She slammed her fist into the doughy mound sending a spray of flour into the air. There was a certain amount of satisfaction in the action. Maybe she ought to recommend it to Kevin as a way to work off tension at the end of a long day at Halloran Industries.

Lacey thought she had the bread under control by the time Kevin came back. She'd actually put the dough into bread pans to rise for the last time. She stood back and admired them, breathing in the yeasty scent. Suddenly she realized she was starved.

"What did you order?" she asked him as he came over to examine the end result of her labors thus far.

"Chow mein, lemon chicken and for you fried rice with shrimp."

"Sounds heavenly."

"I placed another order while I was in there, too," he said, tossing a catalog onto the table. "Check out page five and see what you think."

Lacey's gaze narrowed as she picked up the brochure from a store famous for its kitchenware. She flipped the first couple of pages until she found the item he'd circled: an outrageously expensive automatic bread maker.

"You didn't," she said, laughter bubbling up as she looked at his smug expression.

"I did. If baking bread is going to make you happy, you might as well have the right equipment."

"There are some who'd say this is cheating."

"I prefer to think of it as modernization."

She grinned at him. "I'm not sure your motive is all that altruistic. I suspect you're just hoping I'll convert so you'll have some chance of getting your meals on time."

"Not me," he said piously. "I could live on love."

"I suppose that's why we're having Chinese carryout tonight."

"Exactly. I *love* Chinese carryout."

Lacey caught the devilish twinkle in his eyes and suddenly felt warm all over. In moments like this she felt the deep, abiding pull of her love for Kevin all over again. She knew a lot of women who would regard a kitchen appliance as a sorry excuse for a romantic gift. She also knew that she would always see it as the first concrete evidence that the sensitive, considerate man she'd fallen in love with still existed.

Chapter Nine

Lacey drove into town for a much-needed break from Kevin's gentle attentiveness. After nearly two weeks, she was finding it more and more difficult to ignore her mounting desires and keep her resolve.

Simply wandering the aisles of the grocery store kept her mind on more mundane matters. It was virtually impossible to feel particularly romantic in the frozen food section of the supermarket. It was also good to see other people, many of whom she recognized from past trips.

She had just turned the corner of the canned goods aisle, when she ran into Mrs. Renfield. Dressed in a blue-flowered cotton blouse, a matching sweater the shade of Texas bluebonnets, gray slacks and sensible black shoes, the seventy-five-year-old widow didn't look a day over sixty. There was scarcely a wrinkle on her face, a testament to the floppy-brimmed hat she always wore to work in her garden and to walk on the beach. Though her gray hair looked as if it might have been chopped off with hedge clippers, the short style was actually very becoming.

"Lacey, dear, how wonderful to see you. How did your bread turn out?"

"It was edible," Lacey said ruefully. "But it wasn't nearly as good as yours."

The older woman waved off the compliment. "You'll get the hang of it soon enough. Wouldn't you and Kevin like to drop by for tea this afternoon? I've just made another cherry cobbler. I know how much you both love it. There's even enough for Jason and that new wife of his. Are you expecting them anytime soon?"

"Maybe this weekend, in fact. Kevin mentioned after he talked to Jason this morning that they hoped to drive out on Saturday morning."

"Then you must come by and collect the cobbler. Besides, I haven't seen Kevin once since the two of you came out here."

"I know," Lacey said. "He's been sticking pretty close to home. He's still trying to get his strength back."

"Well, there's nothing better for that than fresh salt air and a brisk walk on the beach. You bring him by for tea and I'll tell him so myself."

Lacey grinned at her. "If I were you, I'd keep my advice to myself. Kevin is getting tired of being told what to do."

"Fiddle-faddle. He can grumble all he wants at me. I can take it. I raised six boys and you'd better believe they all still listen when I have something to say."

"I'm sure they do. I'll see how Kevin's feeling when I get home. I'll call if we can make it over. If not today, soon. I promise."

Mrs. Renfield regarded Lacey intently and patted her hand. "My dear, you mustn't take it to heart when he loses his temper. Men never can deal with being sick. They take it out on whoever's closest to them."

With that reassurance given, the elderly woman was on her way, pushing her grocery cart briskly down the aisle without a backward glance. She was stopped twice more by friends before she reached the end of the row.

How had she known? Lacey wondered. How had a woman she knew only slightly guessed that Kevin was scowling impatiently every time Lacey dared to mention that he was pushing himself too hard?

She shrugged finally. Maybe it wasn't some odd psychic power. Maybe it was simply a matter of understanding the nature of the beast. After all, from the time Jason was old enough to talk, he'd always been a bear, too. He moaned and groaned so pathetically, it might have broken her heart if she hadn't known that he was dealing with a cold or measles and not something fatal. She thought it was poetic justice that he was suffering from morning sickness right along with Dana.

As for Kevin, the worst of it was probably over. Day by day his strength was clearly coming back. After the first week, she had been able to see it in the energy he found to walk on the beach every morning and afternoon. He'd begun to tackle small chores around the house with some semblance of his old enthusiasm.

Lacey might have worried more about the demands he was placing on his still-healing heart, if he hadn't balanced it all with quiet hours of reading. Just last night a techno-thriller had kept him up until the wee hours of the morning. She had seen the light under his door each time she'd awakened. Today at breakfast he'd been anxious to discuss every detail of the fast-paced plot with her.

With Kevin's energy increasing, she wondered how much longer she would be able to keep him idle on the Cape, how much longer before they would have to face making a final decision about their marriage. She knew he'd started making daily phone calls to Brandon and to Jason, though he tried to mask them as nothing more than casual chats. The fact that he felt the need to hide his business calls worried her almost as much as the increasing activity. If he couldn't confide even that, how could they expect to communicate about the really important issues facing them?

When Lacey came home from the store an hour later to find Kevin atop a ladder, clinging to the roof, she felt her heart climb in her throat. As she watched, he saw her and waved, his expression cheerful, his balance at the top of that ladder more precarious than ever.

"I'll be down in a minute," he called as she left the car door open and rushed across the yard to steady the ladder for his descent.

When he finally reached the ground and her own pulse rate slowed to something close to normal, she whirled on him. "Kevin Halloran, are you out of your mind?" Hands on hips, she stood toe-to-toe with him. "What did you think you were doing?"

"Checking the drainpipe for leaves," he replied nonchalantly. He dropped a casual kiss on her forehead. "No big deal."

Lacey felt her temper climb. "No big deal. *No big deal!* You could have fallen and no one would have been here to help. You're not supposed to go up and down steps, much less ladders. What if you'd gotten dizzy?" she demanded, listening to the hysterical rise of her voice, but unable to control it.

"I would have held on until the dizziness passed," he said so calmly that she nearly missed the glint of anger in his eye. "You have to stop hovering over me, Lacey. I can't take much more of it. I won't let you make me out to be an invalid."

She felt as if he'd slapped her. Unshed tears stung her eyes.

"Hovering?" she repeated furiously, Mrs. Renfield's wise advice a distant memory. "Is that what I've been doing? Well, I'm sorry. I thought I was just thinking about your welfare. I thought I was just trying to make sure that you recuperated the way Linc wanted you to. I'm sorry all to hell for worrying about you!"

If she'd had the groceries in her arms, she would have thrown them at him. Instead, she turned and stomped off, only to have him catch her by the arm and twirl her around to meet his equally furious gaze.

Before Lacey could catch her breath, Kevin's lips were on hers, hard and urgent. There was a raw, primitive anger behind the kiss, a battle for possession and control.

She had known the kiss was coming for days now, known that their mutual desire could be banked only so long. She wanted desperately to fight his claim, but her body's needs wouldn't let her. She had hungered for far too long to feel Kevin's mouth on hers, to feel his heat rising, drawing her closer with the certain lure of an old lover. Day by day that hunger had grown, controlled only by stern lectures and rigid willpower.

Now, with the decision taken out of her control, her hands fisted, clinging to the rough denim of his shirt. He dragged her closer until their bodies fit together as naturally as two pieces of a puzzle. Her mouth opened too eagerly for the sweet invasion of his tongue. Within seconds the punishing kiss became a bold, urgent caress that set off a fire low inside her. Her blood rushed to a wilder rhythm.

It had been so long, so terribly long, since she had felt this alluring heat, since his clean, masculine scent had teased her senses. Her responses were instinctive, as doubts and warnings fled. This was the way she and Kevin had once been together—sensual creatures who stirred to passion with the most innocent touch, the most casual glance. This had been the crowning glory of their love, a lure so powerful that nothing, *nothing* could have stood in their way.

Thinking, as she had, that it had been lost, she exhilarated in the sensations pulsing through her body, the quick rise of heat, the questing hunger, the aching need. And all because of a kiss—a single, long, deep, slow kiss.

She moaned as he drew away, moaned and clung to his shoulders, her knees weak, her breathing uneven, her emotions in turmoil.

Reluctant to end the moment, Lacey was slow to open her eyes, slow to search Kevin's expression for some sign of what he was feeling. Even so, it was impossible to miss the naked longing in his eyes, the ragged rise and fall of his chest, the still-angry set to his lips.

"I want you," he said, his voice gruff. "I want you more than I've ever imagined wanting a woman." He took her hand and pressed it against him. "This is what you do to me still, after all this time."

Lacey swallowed hard against the emotions that were crowding in her chest. Her fingers lingered against the roughness of denim, lingered against the evidence of her own powerful sensuality. If she could still affect him like this, if she could still make him yearn to touch and caress and love, weren't all things possible?

Maybe. Maybe not, she thought with a sigh as she slowly withdrew. At her age she knew better than to equate passion with the forever kind of love. Knew better, but wished just the same. Oh, how she wished that these few moments of uncensored desire were proof that she and Kevin were almost there, almost back to the way they had been.

As if the rare display of vulnerability had cost him dearly, Kevin refused to go to Mrs. Renfield's for tea, but insisted Lacey accept the invitation. Lacey went through the motions, listening to the latest gossip, pretending that everything in her own life was fine, accepting the cobbler because it would have hurt the older woman's feelings to turn it down.

When she returned, Kevin was careful to avoid her, as if he feared, as she did, that the raw emotions that had rushed to the surface earlier would disrupt their tenuous hold on an atmosphere of calm.

If they dared to allow passion to run its natural course, would they ever take the time to search their hearts for the answers they needed to make their marriage work? Lacey knew that soul-searching talks were something they had to do. The time was fast approaching when their discussions would have to reach deep, in order to bring all the old hurts into the open. Without such brutally painful honesty, they would never clear the air once and for all.

Lacey spent the last hours of daylight trying to stay out of Kevin's path, not yet ready for a confrontation that would rip open wounds just now healing. Nor was she ready for more of the bittersweet temptation she felt each time he was near—a temptation that taunted all the more now that she knew it was based on reality, not memories.

Kevin retreated emotionally as well as physically. Perhaps, she thought, because his own pride was at stake. He had shown himself to be vulnerable, and she doubted he would allow her to see his need again. Like boxers they had gone to their respective corners to soothe their wounds and prepare for the next round.

That night their unspoken truce was still uneasy. The conversation at dinner was stilted and confined to the barest attempt at politeness. More than once Kevin looked as if he wanted to say something more important than "Pass the pepper," but each time he snapped his mouth closed, leaving the words unsaid. He left the table before dessert, declaring that the cobbler should be saved for Jason and Dana.

Lacey and Kevin sat on opposite sides of the living room, unopened books in their hands, both of them staring at the fire. It was Lacey, nerves unbearably taut, who finally broke the silence.

"I picked up a movie at the video store earlier. Would you like to watch it?"

Kevin shrugged. "We might as well. You put it on. I'll be back in a minute."

When he hadn't returned after a few minutes, she went looking for him. She found him in the kitchen with the refrigerator door open wide. He was scanning the newly filled shelves.

"What are you looking for?" she asked.

"Something to eat while we watch the movie."

She knew what he meant by that. To his way of thinking, carrot sticks, apples and celery were not snacks. A bowl of chocolate chip ice cream, a bigger bowl of buttered popcorn or a handful of crackers with cheddar cheese went with old movies. So did Mrs. Renfield's latest cherry cobbler, which just an hour earlier Kevin had vowed to save. Yet in the midst of a snack attack, she doubted he would remember the promise.

Lacey also knew that she dare not offer advice on the subject of his diet. He'd already indicated what he thought of her interference. She consoled herself with a reminder that Kevin was a grown man. If he was going to improve his health, it would have to be a conscious choice on his part. It was time to let go of her own need to protect him, a need based on her desperate fear of losing him. It was no easier than Jason's first day at school or his departure for college. In so many ways it was more important than either.

Kevin glanced back at her, his expression defensive. "No comment?" he inquired.

"None."

He muttered something under his breath, reached into the refrigerator and withdrew the carrot sticks. Lacey let out the breath she'd been holding. Kevin put a handful of the carrots on a plate, regarded them with disgust and slammed the refrigerator door.

"This better be one helluva a movie," he grumbled as he stalked past her.

"Bogart and Bacall," she reminded him. "How could it be anything else?"

In no time at all Kevin was so absorbed in the film that he didn't even reach for the remaining carrots. Just as Lacey had finally begun to relax, the phone rang. She grabbed it as Kevin cut off the VCR and headed for the kitchen.

"Lacey, it's Paula. Is this a bad time?"

"No, it's fine." Unless Kevin was using it as an excuse to sneak the last of that cobbler, she thought. "What's up?"

"We could really use your help tomorrow. Is there any chance at all you can get to Boston?"

Lacey had a hunch it would be good to allow Kevin some space, more than she'd given him even today. Not only that, she knew she could do with a real break. The nonstop tension of fighting Kevin and her own emotions was beginning to get to her.

"I may be late, but I'll be there," she promised.

"Are you okay? You sound funny," Paula said, quick to pick up on Lacey's mood.

"I'm just tired. I'll get a good night's sleep and be fine by the time I see you."

"If you say so," her friend said skeptically. "Is Kevin okay?"

"Getting better all the time," she responded honestly.

"And you don't intend to say any more than that with him there," Paula replied. "Okay, I'll let you go for now, but be prepared to discuss this in depth to-morrow.''

Lacey's laugh was strained. ''Don't threaten me, pal. I could stay here tomorrow. They're predicting seventy degrees and sunny, a perfect day for the beach.''

''But I know you won't let me down. See you.''

Lacey was slow to hang up. She should tell Kevin about the remarkable housing project in which Paula had involved her. Paula and her husband Dave had never lost the idealistic fervor that had once gripped Kevin and Lacey. Tonight would be the perfect opportunity to fill Kevin in on what their old friends had been doing. Maybe he would even want to ride into town with her, take a look at a project that really worked.

When he hadn't rejoined her ten minutes later, she got up and went to look for him. He wasn't in the kitchen so she walked down the hall and saw that the door to his room was closed.

She opened it a crack. ''Kevin,'' she said softly, as worry sneaked up on her.

After a moment's silence, during which all she heard was the quickened beating of her own heart, he said, ''Yes?''

''Are you okay?''

''Just tired,'' he answered tersely.

His tone concerned her almost as much as the admission. "You're sure that's all it is?"

"Yes. Good night, Lacey."

There was no doubt that he had dismissed her.

"Good night, Kevin," she said, an unmistakable strain in her voice. She sighed and reluctantly closed the door.

She tried watching the rest of the old movie, but couldn't keep her attention focused on the flickering black and white images. Finally she gave up.

In her own room, with the book she'd been reading discarded, she stared at the ceiling and wondered how they could possibly hope to salvage their marriage when more often than not they treated each other like strangers, no doubt because neither of them dared to force the issues they really needed to resolve. Instead they skirted their problems, like drivers avoiding dangerous potholes.

No more, she vowed with determination—most likely because she knew already that tomorrow offered yet another reprieve. She would use the time in Boston to think through the best way to broach things with Kevin. She would organize her thoughts, if not her emotions.

Her plan decided, Lacey tried to sleep. Unfortunately the emotions she'd vowed to dismiss wouldn't release their hold so easily. Every sigh of the wind, each creak of the bedsprings, every crash of waves was enough to bring her wide awake again.

And awake, Kevin's face was always there, and the memories of his caresses were as tantalizing as the reality.

When dawn broke at last, she couldn't wait to run.

Chapter Ten

After the unending tension of the previous evening and the sleepless night, swinging a hammer actually felt good to Lacey. Admittedly she was doing it with more energy than accuracy, but she relished the pull on her muscles, the warmth of the sun on her shoulders.

All around her were the sounds of electric saws, hammers and the blare of sixties rock 'n' roll. The hammering seemed to take on the rhythm of the music.

Simply being among a group that was mostly strangers made it easier not to think about Kevin. During their time on Cape Cod, there had been too many bold glances that unnerved her, too many innocent caresses that tempted, too many whispered words designed to lure.

Especially yesterday. That kiss had very nearly been her undoing. Lacey felt as if she'd been walking a tightrope, trying to maintain her equilibrium above a sea of temptations.

Now with sweat beading on her brow and tracking between her breasts, she put all of those confusing sensations out of her mind to concentrate on the task at hand. It was either that or risk slamming the hammer on her thumb instead of hitting the nails she was supposed to drive into place in the drywall. She'd already done that twice. The result was a throbbing, black and blue thumb, but she was determined not to quit until her assigned section of the house was complete. She knew how anxiously some family was waiting for the day they could move in.

When Paula Gethers had called months ago and pleaded with her to pitch in on a unique housing project that would ultimately provide renovated, low-income homes, the concept had intrigued Lacey. And the timing couldn't have been better. She had just left Kevin, and her days were filled with endless hours of loneliness and regrets.

When Paula had said she didn't want Lacey to do fund-raising, didn't want her to write a check, Lacey had regarded her skeptically.

"What then?"

"I need you to hit nails, paint, maybe lay some tiles. Who knows, maybe I'll have you learn to install plumbing."

Lacey had burst out laughing at that. "You've got to be kidding."

Paula had shaken her head. "Nope. Come take a look."

Lacey had gone that day and been relegated to wielding a paintbrush. She'd ended up with more paint in her hair and on her clothes than on the walls, but she'd been hooked.

The calls had come steadily after that until Lacey was involved almost as closely with the project as her old friend. Last night's call had been more welcome than all the others because it provided her with an excuse to put that much-needed space between herself and Kevin.

At one time she had been on a dozen different committees, all of them demanding, all of them worthwhile. With none of them, though, had she felt such an immediate sense of satisfaction. Never before had she been able to stand back at the end of the day and look at the results of her labors and see so clearly that her contribution of time and energy truly made a difference for some family. Lacey felt good knowing that each house might become a first home for a family previously relegated to a ramshackle public-housing project.

Admittedly there had also been a sense of poignancy. Maybe if such a program had existed years ago, there would have been help for her own family. They had lived in a cramped, run-down, rented apartment, unable to afford anything better, yet too well-off to qualify for assistance.

Lacey would never forget the first time she had gone home with Kevin. She had circled the huge Halloran home as if it were a museum, studying the paintings in Brandon's collection with a sense of awe. The furnishings were perfect, down to the last crystal vase and the matching gold lighter and cigarette case. It was the first time she had truly realized how very different their lives were, and it had terrified her.

For weeks after the visit, she had tried to break things off, tried to put some distance between them. Kevin would have none of it. Intuitively he had known how she felt and even at eighteen he had been determined.

To her horror, he had spoken to her mother and wrangled an invitation to her home for dinner. There, amidst the garage-sale collection of furnishings and the strong aroma of garlic, he had looked as out of place as a Renoir amidst paintings on velvet.

If he had been appalled, though, he hid it well. He had been lavish with his praise of her mother's cooking. With the composure of someone who'd been brought up with all the social graces, he had talked about unemployment with her father, an assembly line worker who feared each and every day would be his last on the job.

Slowly Lacey had relaxed as his charm had touched them all. The evening had been a resounding success. Only later had she realized that that night had been the start of Kevin's transition from being solely her protector to his commitment to broader change for society itself. His fervor had ignited her own and they both had developed a sense of purpose that was all the stronger because it was something they shared.

How long ago that all seemed now. Lacey tugged at the red bandana she'd tied around her neck and pulled it free, then used it to mop her brow. If Kevin could only see her now, she thought. He wouldn't believe the streaks of dirt, the paint and sawdust that clung to her hair, the aching muscles that were proof that on this project at least she was pulling her own weight.

She wasn't sure why she hadn't forced the issue last night and told him where she intended to spend the day. Because he'd slipped away during her conversation with Paula, then taken refuge in his room, she had felt more defeated than she had in a long time. When he'd dismissed her at the doorway, she'd consoled herself that there would be time to explain in the morning.

But when morning came, she had been almost relieved to discover that he was still asleep. Rather than

waking him, she'd left an innocuous note on the
kitchen table beside a bowl of high-fiber cereal.

"Had to go into town. Back by dinner. L."

A zillion years ago, he would have known where she
was going, would have cared about a project like this,
would have been among the first to volunteer. Her
subconscious decision to keep it to herself now spoke
volumes about how she felt his priorities had changed.

Or, more likely, how she feared his reaction would
disappoint her. If he showed no interest or, worse yet,
if he belittled the effort, it would be irrefutable proof
of how much he had changed.

Maybe she was selling him short, though. Maybe if
she gave him a chance, he would share in her excitement. There was only one way to find out. She vowed
then and there to tell him every detail over dinner. And
if his response was only to pull out his pen and write a
check, at least the cause would benefit.

"When was the last time you actually hit a nail?"
Paula inquired, her low, throaty voice filled with
amusement. She sounded as if she ought to do sultry
voice-overs for commercials, rather than spend her
days on a construction site. "If everyone worked at
this rate, the house wouldn't be ready until next year,"
she said.

Lacey glanced at her old friend and laughed. "What
can I say? Volunteer help starts slacking off when the
sun goes down."

"We're a good hour from sunset, lady." Paula handed her a soft drink and settled on the bottom rung of a ladder. "You okay? You looked lost in thought, a little sad."

"I was just wondering what Kevin would think if he could see me now."

"Probably that you'd lost your marbles. That's what Dave thinks about me, and he's been right here every day. He still can't believe that a woman who used to get her nails done twice a week when she was in high school now has none and isn't hysterical over it." She held up her hands, displaying the blunt-cut nails that were free of polish. Tiny cuts and specks of paint had turned them into a worker's hands. "They may not be as pretty, but I figure I've earned every battle scar."

She regarded Lacey closely. "Why haven't you told Kevin about this?"

"I'm not sure," Lacey admitted. "I was just thinking that I'd tell him tonight."

"You might have a glass of brandy nearby in case he swoons from shock the way Dave did. Or you could just bring him by sometime," she suggested slyly. "That's how I sold Dave and you and just about everyone else who's gotten involved."

Lacey grinned. "A pretty sneaky trick, if you ask me."

"I'll use whatever it takes if it means getting these houses fixed up faster. I've fine-tuned my approach to the contractors so they start saying yes when they see me coming. You should have heard the number I pulled on the mayor. I've never been more eloquent, if I do say so myself."

"Has he committed any city funds yet?"

Paula shook her head. "I'm not counting on the city for anything. This is all about private citizens helping each other. I wanted him to cough up his own bucks and a few weekends of his time. I figured he'd be the ideal role model for all the other politicians and give this program some much-needed visibility."

"Did he agree?"

"It's an election year. Just imagine the photo opportunities," she said dryly. She glanced at her watch. "If you're going back out to the Cape tonight, you'd better get started. It will be dark soon and we'll have to shut down for the night, anyway."

Lacey nodded. "I'll try to get back later in the week, by next weekend for sure."

"Who knows? Maybe you'll have Kevin along."

"Yes. Who knows," she said, but she couldn't mask her very real doubts.

If the furious expression on Kevin's face when she drove up was any indication, Lacey figured she'd better not count on him for much of anything. As she crossed the lawn, he opened the screen door and stepped outside.

When she was close enough, he waved her note under her nose. "What is this?"

She immediately bristled at his curt tone. "The note I left for you."

"Is this supposed to give me the first clue about where to find you? What if there'd been an emergency? What if I'd wanted to get in touch with you? Was I supposed to call all over Boston and hope I lucked out?"

She stopped in mid-step and studied him, worry washing through her. "Was there an emergency? Are you okay?"

"Dammit, this is not about my health. It's about your lack of consideration. It's about your running off without so much as a word to let me know where you were going and when you'd be back."

Lacey swallowed the angry retort that rose automatically to her lips. Maybe now he would know how she felt more often than not, shut out and filled with loneliness and longing.

"Well," he demanded, "what do you have to say for yourself?"

"Nothing," she said softly. "You're obviously too upset to listen to reason."

"Don't you dare patronize me."

"We'll discuss it over dinner," she said with deliberate calm as she left him standing in the front hall.

"Oh, no," he said, catching up with her in the doorway to the kitchen and moving quickly into her path. "We'll discuss it *now.*"

Lacey drew in a deep breath and lifted her gaze to clash with his. "Kevin, for the past decade you have not once beat me home in the evenings. I have always left a note just in case. Today I did the same thing. I told you I had gone out, and I told you when I'd be home. I figured you wouldn't be any more interested in the details than you usually are."

Despite her best efforts, she hadn't been able to keep the bitterness out at the end. He looked stunned.

"Not interested?" he repeated softly. "I'm always interested in everything you do."

"No," she said evenly. "That was true once, but not recently. As long as I was there to greet you every evening, as long as I never disrupted your plans, you never once asked a question about how I spent my days."

"I assumed you went to those meetings," he muttered defensively.

"*Those meetings,* as you refer to them, were a sorry substitute for having any real purpose in my life. I know that I am as much to blame for allowing that to happen as you are, but the fact of the matter is that for too long now I have been frustrated, lonely and bored to tears. While you've been climbing the corporate ladder of success, I've been searching for some niche I could fill. Thanks to Paula, I've found it.''

For an instant he looked puzzled. Puzzlement slowly turned to incredulity. ''Paula Gethers? The one who used to organize peace marches? I didn't know the two of you even saw each other anymore.''

''Actually we see each other quite a lot. I'm helping her to renovate houses.''

Kevin's mouth dropped open. ''You're what?'' he asked, not even trying to hide his astonishment and disbelief.

''Renovating houses,'' she repeated a bit more emphatically.

''You mean hiring contractors, decorators, that sort of thing?''

''No. I mean picking up hammers and paintbrushes and screwdrivers.'' She held out her hands for his inspection.

He took her hands and examined them, slowly taking in the specks of paint that had escaped her cleaning, the blister on one finger, the black and blue under the nail of her thumb.

''My God,'' he breathed softly, as he gently smoothed his fingers over the rough spots. ''You're serious, aren't you?''

Lacey withdrew her hand before his touch made her forget how irritated she was. "Never more so," she said with a hint of defiance.

"But why? You could hire anyone you wanted to do that sort of work."

"Not for this. There's no money involved. The work is done by volunteers. The materials are donated. Then the houses are turned over to needy families. Paula's more familiar with the financial arrangements made with the families, but I do know they have to help with the construction."

The last traces of anger vanished from Kevin's eyes. Lacey could tell the exact instant when his imagination caught fire. Her breath caught in her throat. A radiant burst of hope spilled through her.

"Sit down and tell me," he said, urging her to the table. He poured them each a cup of coffee and sat down opposite her. "How does it work? Who's involved?"

Kevin's sudden burst of enthusiasm was catching, reminding her of long-ago nights when they had sat just like this for hours on end. Her words tumbled over each other as she shared her excitement about the program with him. All the things she had longed to describe to him for so long came pouring out.

"I was there the day they turned over the first house I'd worked on," she said. "A single mother was moving in with her three kids. There were tears in her eyes as she walked from room to room just touching things. She said she'd never before seen anyplace so clean."

Tears welled up in Lacey's eyes as she remembered that day. "Oh, Kevin, if only you could have been there. Knowing that that house was hers filled her with so much pride and so much determination. You could see it in her face. This is the kind of social program that really works, that doesn't spend a fortune on overhead. It gets down to one of the very first basics of life, shelter."

"I want to see for myself," Kevin said when she was finally done. He got up and began to pace, just as he always had when he was trying to work out a complex problem. "Maybe there's some way Halloran can get involved," he said finally. "We could donate fabric for draperies, underwrite some of the costs to buy up land or old houses. What do you think? Would that help?"

Lacey felt a wellspring of emotion rise up inside her. *This* was the Kevin she'd fallen in love with. *This* was the man who was touched by the plight of others and wanted desperately to help.

"Thank you," she said, feeling as if a boulder had lodged in her throat.

He seemed puzzled by her emotion. "Lacey, it's only some fabric and a few dollars. Halloran makes donations like that all the time."

She shook her head. "You're wrong. It's much more."

"I don't understand."

"Kevin, it's more proof that the man I fell in love with still exists. Don't you see? If we could work together on this, it would be a start, a new beginning for us."

As understanding dawned, he clasped her hands in his and lifted them to his mouth. He kissed each speck of paint, each blemish until Lacey was sure the earth was falling away beneath her. She wanted to fling her arms around him, wanted to welcome him back from the cold, uncaring, distant place it seemed he'd gone without her. She held back only by reminding herself that this was only a beginning.

They were up until midnight making plans. Dinner was no more than sandwiches hastily slapped together and eaten distractedly. When neither of them could hold their eyes open a minute longer, they were still reluctant to go to bed. In the hallway between their rooms, their gazes caught and held.

Lacey raised her fingers to caress his cheek. "I love you," she dared to say for the first time in months.

"And I love you," he echoed. He glanced toward the door of the master bedroom, then back to her. "Lace?"

Her heart hammered in her chest at the invitation. To spend the night in his bed again, in his arms, would be just this side of heaven. But something inside her whispered that it was still too soon, that to give in to the provocative promise in his eyes would risk everything.

"I can't," she said finally.

She saw the quick hurt in his eyes and wished she could take the words back, but it was too late. Already he was retreating.

How many more times could she bring herself to say no? she wondered. How many more times could Kevin hear it without distancing himself from her for good? Would she even know when it was time to put her heart and soul on the line, no matter what?

The elusive answer to those questions kept her awake most of the night. When the early morning hours came, the questions were still there. And the answers were no clearer.

Chapter Eleven

So many times during the night Kevin was tempted to get up and go across the hall. It was three o'clock when he knew he could no longer deny himself. Lacey was still his wife. He still loved her with all his heart. And he knew in his gut that the longer they allowed this foolishness of separate bedrooms to go on, the more difficult it would be to end.

The longing in Lacey's eyes tonight had been unmistakable. Whatever was holding her back mystified him. She wasn't the type to play games. She never had been. Even when they had made love for the very first time, there had been no coy pretenses between them.

His thoughts drifted back to that long-ago night. It had been here on Cape Cod, the summer after their freshman year in college. Vacation was almost over and they faced another long year of being apart, thanks to his father's determined interference.

They had come to the beach for the weekend with friends, but had quickly abandoned them in favor of privacy. They had gone for a walk on the beach, their way lit by the full moon. When they found a secluded cove, he had spread a blanket on the still-warm sand. Other nights, other summers, they had done no more than sit and talk, often until dawn, but somehow both of them knew that this night would be different. The love that had blossomed between them with a slow, sweet dawning needed expression in a new and exciting way.

Lacey had made the first bold move. With his eyes riveted on her, she had slowly removed her clothes. She had been a virgin, yet there had been no shyness in her that night. She had stood before him, naked in the moonlight, proud, her eyes filled with love.

"Make love to me," she had whispered.

Uncertain, he was the one to hesitate. He had always been so sure that he was the stronger one, but that night Lacey had proved him wrong. She had been bold and daring, while he thought his heart would split in two with the sheer joy of making her his.

Slowly, tenderly he had claimed her, enchanted by the velvet softness of her flesh, intoxicated by the taste of her. He had wanted her for so long, needed her forever it seemed. His hands trembled as they cupped her breasts. His pulse raced as he touched her moist warmth. She had been so hot, so ready for him, so eager to guide him into her.

As he sank into her that very first time, she had cried out his name, not in pain as he had feared, but in unmistakable exhilaration. Surrounded by her heat, thrilled by her pleasure, he had felt his own pleasure build and build until he too came apart in a shattering climax that was beyond anything he had ever imagined.

Just thinking about it now aroused him to a state of breathless, aching anticipation. It was past time for patience, past time for half measures. He stood up and crossed the room in three strides. At the door he hesitated, then shook off his doubts. No, he was right about this. He had to be.

He paused again at the guest room door, then opened it slowly. Inside, a beam of moonlight streamed through the window casting a silvery glow over Lacey's complexion. She was wearing a gown of French lace and Halloran's finest pale pink satin. It was one he had given to her for their last anniversary. Though she preferred a classic, elegant look in public, she had always loved impractical, frothy concoctions for sleeping. In this one, she looked more feminine, more tantalizing than ever.

Tenderness welled up inside him, as he guessed how restless she had been. The sheets were in a tangle. The gown had ridden up to bare one glorious, tempting thigh. Kevin sucked in a ragged breath as desire pulsed through him. She was so incredibly beautiful, so inviting.

And so exhausted, he realized as he inched closer and glimpsed the shadows under her eyes. It was little wonder after the day she had spent working with Paula...and after the torment he had put her through for far longer than that.

Honor warred with need. This time, to his regret, honor won.

Reluctantly Kevin settled for a whisper-light caress of her shoulder, as he shifted one fallen strap of her gown back into place. Fingertips skimmed over cool, silken flesh, lingered as his pulse skipped, then raced.

Lacey's breath hitched at the touch. He held his own breath in an agony of anticipation, waiting to see if she would wake, hoping against hope that she would. He told himself he would be blameless then.

When she didn't awaken, when the pattern of her breathing became slow and steady again, he sighed.

Tomorrow, he promised himself. Tomorrow they would find their way back into each other's arms.

* * *

Lacey spent the morning trying to figure out why Kevin suddenly seemed so nostalgic. It was as if he'd spent the whole night lost in memories, caught up in the same sweetly tormenting dreams that she had had when she'd finally fallen into a restless slumber.

Today it seemed as if he were using those memories to rekindle the desire that had always surged between them like a palpable force.

"What's gotten into you?" she murmured, when his hand curved around the nape of her neck for just an instant as he returned to the breakfast table. The casual touch sent her pulse scrambling. She tried to cover it by spreading jam on her toast.

"I don't know what you mean," he said, pouring himself a second cup of coffee, his expression all smug male innocence.

She regarded him with disbelief, then finally shrugged. "Perhaps it's just my imagination playing tricks with me."

He nodded, rather quickly she thought.

"I'm sure that's it," he agreed, but the gleam in his eyes contradicted the too-casual response.

Her gaze narrowed. "Are you sure you have no idea what I'm talking about?"

His eyes widened. "None. Did you sleep well?"

"I tossed and turned a bit. You?"

"I was a bit restless myself. I looked in on you," he said in a voice that sounded a bit husky.

Surprised, she didn't know what to say, finally settling for a simple, "Oh?"

She reached hurriedly for a section of the Boston paper so she could hide the flush of embarrassment that she could feel creeping into her cheeks. Kevin nudged the paper aside.

"Lacey." His voice was soft and slow as honey, but it held a definite note of command.

She swallowed hard, then forced herself to meet his gaze. "Yes?"

"You looked very beautiful."

This time there was no hiding the heat that climbed into her cheeks. "Kevin Halloran, if I didn't know better, I'd think you were trying to rattle me."

He grinned at that. "Then you obviously don't know me at all. Actually my intentions aren't nearly that honorable. I want to seduce you."

Lacey felt every muscle in her body clench, not just at his words, though those were disturbing enough, but at the spark of satisfaction in his eyes.

"Am I having any luck?" he asked, his tone light.

"The offer is tempting," she admitted.

"That's good."

"It is the middle of the morning, though."

"And what is wrong with making love to my wife in the middle of the morning?"

"Not a thing," she murmured breathlessly, captivated by the possibilities.

She saw his whole body tense at that. He held out his hand. She was about to reach for it when reason intruded. There were a hundred reasons for going to bed with Kevin and a thousand more for saying no. She had remembered them all last night. Today it seemed she had to search her memory for just one.

"We can't, Kevin," she said desperately, thinking of Linc's insistent warning. "It's too soon."

Sudden anger turned his eyes a stormy shade of gray blue. "Too soon?" he repeated in a voice that throbbed with sarcasm. "Too soon for whom? We haven't made love in a year. Maybe more."

Though he had missed her meaning entirely, Lacey was too stunned by his harsh, bitterly accusing tone to explain. Instead, she snapped back, "And whose fault is that? Not mine, dammit. I wasn't the one who spent sixteen hours a day in an office and came home exhausted. I'm not the one who was so caught up in work that nothing else mattered."

"No," he said, his tone and his gaze as cold as a winter morning. "You were the one who walked out."

At that she shoved her chair back from the table and forced herself to be silent. Arguing was no solution. If anything it would only make matters worse. But all of this tiptoeing around their problems for fear of upsetting Kevin was beginning to get to her. How many times could she clamp her mouth shut, holding in her hurt, her anger?

At the sink, Lacey gripped the edge of the counter so tightly her knuckles turned white. She drew in a deep, calming breath before she turned back to face him.

"We have to talk about all of this, but only when we can do it calmly."

"I'm not feeling one damn bit calm," he said furiously. "I am sick and tired of being made out to be the bad guy here. I'm a human being, Lacey. Not some storybook hero. I'm sure I've made more than my share of mistakes, but so have you." He glared at her. "So, my dear, have you."

Before Lacey could gather her wits for a comeback, Kevin was gone, leaving her alone with her anger and with the sad awareness that after all these days together, they were not one bit better off than they had been months ago. They didn't understand each other at all anymore.

Lacey was still in the kitchen, lingering over a last cup of coffee, when she heard a car pull up outside. She heard Kevin open the door and she wandered into the hallway to see who'd come to visit.

Jason and Dana. Dear Lord, she had forgotten they were coming. She viewed their arrival as a mixed blessing. They would serve as a buffer after this morning's angry exchange. At the same time, their presence would create even more tension as she and Kevin both struggled to keep their son and daughter-in-law from seeing how little progress had actually been made toward a reconciliation.

As they hurried inside with their bags, Lacey was all too aware of the anxious glances they exchanged.

"Hi, Mom," Jason said, his voice too cheerful. His gaze searched her face. "You've gotten a little sun."

"I've been gardening," she said, putting her cup down to hug Jason and then Dana. She smiled at her daughter-in-law. "How are you feeling?"

"Much better. Jason's finally stopped getting morning sickness."

"Thank goodness," he murmured fervently.

"All men should have a taste of what it's like to carry a baby," Dana retorted. "It might make them more sympathetic."

"I'm sympathetic, all right. But we're only having the one. I can't go through this again."

"You!" Dana retorted indignantly. "At least you'll miss out on the labor pains."

Lacey decided she'd better step in before the familiar battle worsened. "Enough, you two. Where's Sammy?"

"We left him with Brandon," Dana said. "Sammy said something about teaching him to shoot down some kind of creatures."

"A video game created by a sadistic computer hack," Jason explained. "I was awake until three in the morning trying to save some princess from those same evil guys. They multiply like rabbits if you don't stay on your toes."

"Sounds intriguing," Lacey said. "You'll have to teach your father sometime."

"Not while he's recuperating," Dana warned. "It turns them into glassy-eyed monsters. I'm sure it can't be good for their blood pressure. I dared to interrupt Sammy and Jason for dinner the other night and they both jumped down my throat."

"I was winning for the first time in history," Jason explained. "I wasn't about to lose my competitive edge."

Dana rolled her eyes. "See what I mean?"

Jason put an arm around her waist and hugged her. "I love you, anyway," he said. "Where should I put our bags? The guest room across from yours and Dad's?"

Kevin deliberately turned away, leaving Lacey to respond. "No," she said, all too aware of the puzzled expression on Dana's face and on Jason's. There was no hiding the truth from them, though.

"Actually, my things are in there," she said briskly. "Use the yellow room at the end of the hall. It has the second best view in the house."

Jason shot her a sharp look, but fortunately he didn't make an issue of it. He picked up the bags. "I'll be right back. Dana, please go sit down."

"I've been sitting down," she reminded him very patiently. She regarded Lacey hopefully. "He will get over this, won't he?"

"Kevin never did. He watched me like a hawk all during the entire pregnancy. So did Brandon. It almost drove me wild."

"Fortunately Sammy and I made a pact. He'll keep Brandon busy and I will buy him the latest video games. Hopefully they won't release too many new ones between now and when this little one is born."

She patted her rounded belly. "Do you think there's any chance at all I'll have a girl?" she asked wistfully. "I would sure like to buy dolls, instead of footballs."

"The Halloran genes are against it," Kevin said. "I have to admit, though, that I wouldn't mind having a little girl to spoil rotten."

"There will be no spoiling of this child, girl or boy," Dana said firmly.

Lacey shook her head. "Then you married into the wrong family. The Halloran men take spoiling for granted, especially when it comes to grandchildren. I remember the first Christmas after I met Kevin. His grandfather was still alive then. He gave him the first ten-thousand-dollar installment on his trust fund."

"As I recall, I wasn't that impressed," Kevin countered. "I wanted a new ten-speed bike."

"That's okay. I was awed enough for both of us. I got a sweater and a doll that year. They were both second-hand."

Kevin smiled at her, his eyes gentle and filled with remembering. "You still have that doll, though, don't you? While I gave that money away long ago."

"To buy toys for the Salvation Army's Christmas drive," Lacey recalled. "You'd just turned twenty-one, which meant you could start drawing on the trust. I thought using the money to buy those toys was the sweetest thing you'd ever done."

"Dad thought I'd taken leave of my senses. You were six months pregnant and I was giving away our savings to charity." He shook his head. "Talk about irresponsible."

"I didn't think it was irresponsible," Lacey argued. "We had enough. Those people didn't have anything."

"I agree with Lacey," Dana said, leaning down to give Kevin a kiss on his forehead. "It was a noble gesture."

Kevin reached up and patted her cheek. "That's all it was, a gesture. It didn't really solve anything."

Lacey lost patience. "It gave those families and kids a decent holiday, one they'll always remember. If more people made gestures like those, the world would be a better place. What's happened to you, Kevin? When did you become so cynical?''

"Cynical? No, Lacey. I grew up.''

She was about to argue, when she saw the alarm in Dana's eyes. She bit back a sharp retort and shrugged. "I guess we still see some things differently,'' she said and stood up. "I think I'll get busy on lunch. Dana would you like to help me?''

Her daughter-in-law cast one last confused look at Kevin, then followed Lacey into the kitchen.

"Things aren't any better, are they?'' Dana said as they prepared lunch.

"Better?'' Lacey echoed with a catch in her voice. "If anything, they're worse than ever.''

"But why? I don't understand. Anyone who looks at the two of you can see how much you still love each other.''

Lacey shrugged. "When you get right down to it, love may not conquer all.''

"Now who's sounding cynical?'' Dana asked too gently.

Lacey had to fight off the tears that suddenly threatened. She tried to smile. "Come now, you didn't drive all the way out here just to be depressed. Let's have some lunch and then you and Jason can go for a walk on the beach. It's a beautiful day.''

Dana looked as if she wanted to say more, but finally she took her cue from Lacey and busied herself with the lunch preparations.

They all ate much too quickly, anxious to put an end to the charade of cheer they tried to maintain. Jason had barely put his last bite of food in his mouth, when Dana stood up and grabbed his hand. "Let's take a walk."

Startled, he simply stared at her. "Before dessert?"

"Yes," she said firmly. With a shrug, he left the table and followed her from the room.

Kevin glanced across the table, his expression rueful. "I'll bet they can't wait to get back to Boston."

Lacey nodded. "I can't say that I blame them."

He hesitated, then finally looked straight into her eyes. "Do you want to leave, too? Was all of this a mistake?"

A sigh of regret shuddered through her as she thought about the question. "No," she said at last. "But I think we were expecting too much. We need to talk—" When he started to speak, she held up her hand. "No. I mean really talk. And we can't do that if I'm terrified of upsetting you."

"Is that really the problem?"

"It is a lot of it," she admitted. "Every time I think that I'm ready to bring everything out into the open, I remember the way you looked in that intensive care unit. I caution myself to wait, just a little longer, just until Linc pronounces you fit again."

"Is that what you meant this morning when you said it was too soon for us to make love?" Kevin asked, his expression oddly hopeful.

"Yes. Then you took it wrong and the next thing I knew we were shouting. If only we could do this calmly and rationally, but unfortunately there's too much hurt and anger."

She couldn't miss his sigh of regret at her words. "What's going to happen to us, Lacey?" he said.

"We're going to survive all this," she said with sudden certainty. "If we can face it, if we can finally begin to be open and honest about our feelings, then we'll survive. We just have to be patient."

"Not one of my virtues, I'm afraid."

"No," she agreed with the beginnings of a smile. "But maybe it's time you learned a little about patience, for more reasons than one."

He reached for her hand and this time she took it and held on tight.

"You're the best reason I can think of, Lacey," he said quietly. "The very best."

Lacey felt her heart climb into her throat. "Maybe we should make a pact."

"We seem to be doing a lot of that."

"But this one could be the most important of all."

"What, then?"

"Could we pretend, just for a few days, that everything is okay between us? Maybe that would take the pressure off. As it is, we're too demanding of ourselves. Every conversation turns into some sort of cross-examination or psychoanalysis. Maybe we should just forget about all the problems and just be ourselves, have a little fun. We can save the serious talk for later."

Kevin looked skeptical. "Isn't that a little like hiding from reality?"

Lacey laughed. "It's a *lot* like hiding from reality, but so what? Nobody's on a timetable here, right? There's no law that says we must resolve every last problem by a certain date, is there?"

"I guess not," he said slowly. "I don't suppose this plan of yours includes moving back into the master bedroom?"

She stood up and pressed a kiss to his forehead. "Don't push your luck, pal."

"Medically speaking, you mean?"

His arm curved around her waist and tumbled her into his lap. Lacey gazed up into eyes that were suddenly filled with laughter. Serenity stole through her then, for the fist time in days.

"Medically speaking," she confirmed softly just before Kevin's mouth settled over hers in a kiss that was filled with tenderness and promise.

That was the way Jason and Dana found them, still at the kitchen table, still wrapped in each other's arms.

"This is an improvement," Jason commented approvingly from the doorway.

"Jason," Dana muttered urgently, tugging on his arm. "Leave them alone."

Lacey laughed. "Too late," she said as she stood up. "How about a game? Scrabble? Cards?"

"Cutthroat Scrabble," Kevin said with a hint of his old enthusiasm. They had spent many an evening engaged in just such battles before the age of video games.

Jason looked from his father to Lacey and back again, then nodded in satisfaction. "I'll get the board."

"And I'll get the snacks," Dana said.

Jason groaned. "Don't let her, Mom. The only things she likes these days are pickles and brownies."

Lacey patted her son's cheek. "Don't worry. We're fresh out of both."

"Don't be so sure," Jason retorted. "I'm relatively certain that's what she brought out here in that extra suitcase."

Kevin stood up. "Maybe I ought to get the snacks."

This time it was Lacey who groaned.

Kevin grinned at her. "Calm down, my love. There's enough celery and carrot sticks in the refrigerator to feed an army, to say nothing of one pregnant lady, one recuperating man and two nervous nellies.''

The first word Lacey played on the Scrabble board was *joy*. It might not have earned as many points as some others she could have made, but it was definitely the one that best summed up the way she was feeling as she was surrounded by her family once again.

From the warm, tender expression in Kevin's eyes when he caught her gaze, it was a feeling he understood—and shared.

Chapter Twelve

Having Jason and Dana around did indeed take off the pressure, Kevin realized on Sunday. Witnessing his son and daughter-in-law's happiness spun a web of serenity around all of them.

Slowly he and Lacey had relaxed. Like old friends rediscovering shared interests, their laughter came more easily. And the looks they exchanged were filled with open awareness, rather than carefully banked accusation.

When they stood in the driveway to say goodbye, his arm curved naturally around Lacey's waist. And when Jason's car was out of sight, it seemed just as natural that their hands met and laced together.

"Feel like a walk on the beach?" he asked, reluctant to go back inside and risk spoiling the lazy, spellbinding mood. "We should have another hour or so of daylight."

"A walk sounds good," she said.

At the edge of the yard they slipped off their shoes, then crossed the dunes to reach the water's edge. The last of the day's sunlight slanted across the beach. Much of the wide stretch of sand had been cast in shadow, making the sand cool against their bare feet. For as far as Kevin could see, he and Lacey were alone in the early-evening shadows.

"Isn't this perfect, when it's like this?" Lacey asked with a sigh. "No one around. It's almost possible to believe that we're the only ones who know about this stretch of beach."

"Remind me to bring you back in mid-July," Kevin said, thinking of the crowds that descended with the first full days of summer and remained until Labor Day at least.

"And spoil the illusion? No way."

They walked as far as they could before the tide caught up with them and forced them to turn back. For the first time in months the silence that fell between them was comfortable, rather than strained. Neither of them seemed to feel the need to cover the quiet time with awkward conversation.

Kevin glanced over and caught the slow curving of Lacey's lips. "A penny for your thoughts," he said.

"At today's rate of inflation? You've got to be kidding," she said, repeating a joke that they'd shared over the years whenever one of them tried to pry into the other's secret thoughts.

"How much are your thoughts going for these days?"

She seemed to consider the question carefully. "A hundred dollars easy."

He reached in his back pocket and pulled out his wallet. He found the hundred-dollar bill he'd tucked there and offered it to her. "These thoughts of yours better be good."

"In whose opinion?" she countered, nabbing the money and tucking it into her pocket.

"Mine. Pay up."

She grinned at him with a wicked gleam in her eyes. "Chicken," she said succinctly.

"I beg your pardon?"

"I was thinking about chicken. Do you realize that there are at least a hundred different ways to fix chicken? And that's before you get into the ethnic variations."

Kevin regarded her intently. "I just paid one hundred dollars for a dissertation on chicken recipes?" He held out his hand. "I don't think so. I expected something terribly revealing about your romantic soul. Give the money back. You took it under false pretenses.''

"Try to get it," she challenged and took off running.

Her pace was lightning quick at first as he stood flat-footed and stared after her in delighted astonishment. Then he took off after her. He was aware of the precise moment when she slowed down just enough to be caught. He fell on top of her as they tumbled onto the sand.

"You let me catch you," he accused, all too aware of the press of her breasts against his chest and the familiar fit of their lower bodies. He captured her hands and pinned them over her head. Her eyes were filled with laughter and her breath was coming in soft, ragged puffs that fanned his face.

"Maybe I did and maybe I didn't," she taunted.

"Lacey Grainger Halloran, you are a tease."

She wriggled beneath him, just enough to confirm the accusation. There was an unmistakable flare of excitement in her eyes, though she did her damnedest to look innocent.

"Me?" she murmured.

"Yes, you," he said softly, and then he lowered his mouth to cover hers. Her lips were soft and moist enough to have him forgetting to be sensible and slow and careful. Her mouth tempted, like the lure of a flame, and the heat it sent spiraling through him was devastating.

Their bodies strained together, hers arching into his in a way that had him aching with an arousal so hard, so demanding that he thought it very likely he might embarrass himself as he hadn't since the first time he'd experimented with sex.

Kevin fought for calm by rolling over on his back, taking Lacey with him so that he could see her face and the gathering stars in the evening sky at the same time.

"Good Lord, woman, what you do to me," he murmured, his hands lightly brushing the sand from her face, then lingering to caress.

"I know," she said, her expression dreamy and open for once. "It's the same for me with you. Sometimes you touch me and I think I'll fly apart. It's always been that way."

"Always?" he teased. "In the fifth grade you had the hots for me?"

She laughed at that. "Of course, only then I thought it was an allergy. I had a hunch a doctor could cure it, but I never quite got around to checking."

"Thank God," he said fervently.

"What about you?" she questioned, smoothing her fingers along the curve of his jaw. "Did I make you come unglued in the fifth grade?"

"Only when you hit that home run during the spring baseball tournament. I was ready to marry you after that."

"Fortunately there are laws about that sort of thing."

"I'm glad we waited as long as we did," he said, his hands stroking over the backs of her thighs and up over her still-perfect bottom. Even through a layer of denim, she tempted. "I wouldn't have missed the sweet anticipation of those years for anything."

"Me, neither," she whispered, twining her arms around his neck and fitting her head into the curve of his shoulder. "Me, neither."

They stayed right where they were, snuggled comfortably together, for what seemed an eternity. Neither of them was willing to move and risk losing the rare and special mood. Despite thick sweaters and jeans, they were both cold and damp through to their bones by the time they finally made the effort to stand up and go inside.

"How about soup?" Lacey suggested as they stood in front of the fire to warm up.

"Chicken noodle, no doubt," he said.

She scowled at him, but her eyes were bright with laughter. "I was thinking of that white bean soup you like so much. It's thick and hearty, the perfect thing for a night like this. Of course, I could manage chicken noodle from a can, if that's your preference."

"Is there any of that bread you made left?"

"Yes."

"Then the white bean soup and bread sounds great."

"Here, in front of the fire?"

"Yes."

He followed her into the kitchen and helped with chopping onions and gathering silverware. There was something reassuring and cozy about working side by side to prepare a meal. How long had it been since they had done that? Before he'd hired the housekeeper certainly. And long before that? Maybe so.

Possibly from the first moment he'd gone to work at Halloran, when he'd realized that Lacey didn't really want to hear how his days at his father's company had gone.

Before that, early in their marriage they had both rushed in after six and divided up the chores so they could get dinner on the table at a decent hour. Lacey had cooked. He had set the table. And they had used the time to compare notes on everything they'd done while apart.

Occasionally he had fixed dinner and let her catch up on laundry. Without any particular planning, they had had the ultimate liberated household, Kevin realized now with amusement. Still, the rhythm of their evenings had been satisfying in some elusive way he couldn't begin to explain. There had been a closeness, a unity. How had he forgotten that?

The phone rang just as Lacey was ready to ladle up the soup. "I'll get it," he offered and picked up the receiver.

"Kevin?"

"Hey, Dad, how are you?"

He glanced at Lacey and saw her shoulders stiffen almost imperceptibly.

"Fine, now that that rapscallion of Dana's has gone home. That boy wears me out."

"Are you sure it isn't the other way around? What did you two do all weekend?"

"Played some fool video game. A lot of nonsense, if you ask me."

"You must have lost," Kevin guessed.

"The boy whipped the daylights out of me," his father admitted with an indignant huff. "No respect for his elders."

"You wanted Sammy to let you win?"

"Of course not, but he didn't have to humiliate me."

Brandon cleared his throat, always a prelude to saying something he figured the other person didn't want to hear. Kevin waited, his nerves tensed.

"I didn't call up there to discuss video games," his father announced. "Just wanted to see how things are going."

"*Things,*" he mocked, realizing where the conversation was headed, "are going fine."

"You ready to get back to work?"

"Dad, don't start."

"I'm not pushing, son. Just asking."

"With you, it's hard to tell the difference."

Brandon uttered a long-suffering sigh. "It sure is hard to get an ounce of respect in this family."

Kevin ignored the play for sympathy. Finally his father said, "You and Lacey doing okay?"

Now they were really getting down to the reason for the call. Kevin studied his wife out of the corner of his eye. There was no mistaking the tense set of her shoulders now. It was as if she could hear her father-in-law's end of the conversation, rather than just Kevin's innocuous replies.

"Okay," he said, wondering if he was stretching the truth.

"Hear she was staying across the hall."

"Dad! That is none of your business." Only Lacey's presence kept him from saying more. He would speak to Jason first thing tomorrow about spreading tales, especially to Brandon. Jason had had his own bitter experience with his grandfather's meddling. He should have known better.

"Of course it's my business. Your happiness will always be my concern."

"Drop it," Kevin warned.

"Okay, okay. The papers on that deal for the new looms are due in tomorrow. Shall I send 'em on out there?"

Kevin hesitated. Those papers were likely to be like waving a red flag under Lacey's nose. On the other hand, what harm could there possibly be in looking through a contract? Somebody besides Brandon needed to look at the fine print. His father wanted those new looms too badly to worry about whether they were being taken to the cleaners on the deal.

"Send them out," he said finally. "Dad, I've got to go now. Lacey has dinner ready."

"You give her my love, then," his father said. "And tell her to get the hell back in her own bed where she belongs. Better yet, put her on and I'll tell her myself."

Kevin groaned. "You will do nothing of the kind. Good night, Dad."

When he'd hung up, Lacey put their bowls of soup on trays, along with the warm bread. They carried the meal into the living room and settled down on the sofa in front of the fire.

For the first time in the last twenty-four hours the silence that fell between them was uneasy. Kevin was more disappointed than surprised.

"Okay," he said finally, putting his spoon down carefully. "What's on your mind?"

"Who says anything is on my mind?" Lacey asked stiffly.

"Lacey, being evasive won't help anything."

"Okay, what did Brandon want this time?"

"He just called to say hello."

She regarded him doubtfully. "It certainly took him long enough to spit one word out."

"You know what I meant," Kevin said, his irritation beginning to mount. "What is it with you and my father? I thought all that animosity was a thing of the past. I thought you'd forgiven him years ago."

"I did."

"Then why do you react like this every time he calls up?"

"He's trying to get you to start working again, isn't he? Doesn't he realize that the whole purpose of your coming out here was to recuperate?"

With her gaze pinned on him, he couldn't manage a convenient lie. "It's just some papers. It'll take me an hour or two."

"Just some papers. An hour or two," Lacey repeated. "Can't you see that's just the tip of the iceberg with Brandon? Next he'll be pulling up here with an attaché case filled with more papers and a fax machine."

"So what if he does?" Kevin snapped. "I have to get back to work sooner or later. I'll be a helluva lot more relaxed here than I would be back in Boston."

Lacey didn't respond to that.

Kevin threw down his napkin. "On second thought, maybe Boston would be simpler. I wouldn't have to worry about you looking over my shoulder making judgments, would I?"

He stood up and started for the door. "I'm going for a walk."

"Kevin," Lacey called after him.

The last thing he heard before he slammed the front door was her muttered curse.

"Damn," Lacey muttered for the tenth time as she paced and waited for Kevin to come back. How had a simple phone call reopened every wound and shattered the cautious tranquility they had finally managed to achieve?

Because it had been from Brandon, of course. She had heard more than enough to realize he had work for Kevin to do. If she hadn't guessed, Kevin's guilty expression would have told her. She suspected there was more—probably unwanted advice about their marriage, if she knew Brandon.

Even so, it had been stupid to force the issue with Kevin. She couldn't keep jumping down his throat over every little thing.

What on earth was wrong with her? Was she so terrified of losing him that she wanted to wrap him in a cloak of that protective bubble wrap and watch over him for the rest of their lives? What kind of life would that be for either of them? Longer, maybe, but rife with tension.

She was going to have to get a grip on herself. She was going to have to ignore her obviously futile plan to hold reality at bay and start talking. No matter how much the words hurt. No matter how angry they got. They could not allow their pain to fester any longer. Tonight had been proof of that. After a wonderful day of pretending that everything was normal again in their marriage, they had slammed into reality with one phone call.

Lacey was waiting in the living room when Kevin finally came in. She heard him start down the hall and called out to him. For an instant she was afraid he would ignore her, but finally she heard a cautious movement, then a quiet, "Yes?"

"Will you join me?"

"I don't think so," he said. "I'm tired. I'm going to bed."

"Please, Kevin."

"Why, Lacey? What's the point?"

"Our marriage is the point."

"Right now I don't give our marriage a snowball's chance in hell," he said with bleak finality. "Maybe

I'll have a different view in the morning, but I wouldn't hold my breath, if I were you.''

He was gone before she could force a single word past the tears that clogged her throat.

Chapter Thirteen

All the pretense, all the games had to end, Lacey reminded herself as she sat at the kitchen table in the morning. She had made a pot of tea and laced it liberally with milk. She didn't need the jagged edginess of too much caffeine on top of everything else today. Her nerves were already shot and it was barely six a.m.

She could hear the first faint sounds of the birds as dawn finally broke beyond the horizon. Black became gray, then purple, then softest pink as the sun edged its way up through the clouds. This was her favorite time of day, a time when anything seemed possible. She needed that sense of hope more than ever as she waited for Kevin to join her.

Lacey thought of all the emotions she'd kept hidden, all the desperate thoughts she had never dared to voice, and tried to pick one above all the others as a place to start.

It would be so much easier if healing could take place without all this airing of past betrayals, she thought wistfully. But it would be false healing, one that could never last.

Above all else, she wanted whatever happened today to be the beginning of forever. Her marriage would be salvaged today.

Or it wouldn't.

Either way, she would go on. Both of them would. They were too strong not to fight for happiness—together or apart.

Kevin was wide awake when he heard Lacey leave her room and go into the kitchen. It was still dark outside, too early to be up on a vacation day, far too early to begin dealing with anything that required soul-searching.

But this was no normal vacation, he reminded himself wearily. He couldn't begin to recall the last time he had taken one of those. As for soul-searching, what difference did it make if he went over and over things here in his head or voiced them aloud to Lacey?

Even so, as he lay on the bed, his hands behind his head, he was struck by an odd reluctance to get up and see what form their confrontation was likely to take. After last night, he doubted they would have anything pleasant to say to each other. There was the heavy sense of impending doom weighing him down. He no longer had any idea whether the fault for that was Lacey's or his own. He just knew, as he expected she did, that they couldn't go on this way.

He'd expected something simple to come of this trip, something magical. Instead he'd been faced with a hard dose of reality. For a man who prided himself on having outgrown so many naive attitudes, he'd clung to this one about his marriage for far too long.

He heard the whistle of the teakettle, a sure sign that Lacey's distress was as deep and dark as his own. She drank tea only when she needed comfort. He could visualize her sitting at the kitchen table, an old china cup cradled in her hands, her gaze fixed on the splashy display of daybreak, her thoughts...

Well, who knew where her thoughts were? He definitely didn't anymore, not with any certainty.

How he regretted that, he thought with a sigh. He regretted too damned much these days, it seemed.

Then fix it, a voice inside his head muttered. *Fix it now or forget it.*

With understandable reluctance, Kevin finally dragged himself out of bed and pulled on a comfortable pair of soft, well-worn jeans and a fisherman's knit sweater that he and Lacey had bought years ago on a trip to Ireland. He dragged on socks and sneakers, because of the chill in the air, though he would have preferred to be barefoot.

He took as long as he could brushing his teeth and shaving. He even ran a comb through his hair. It was a delaying tactic more than anything. His hair had always fallen where it damn well pleased, unless he tamed it often with a short cut. It had grown past taming over the last few weeks and there was too much silver amidst the blond. Funny how there were days when he truly forgot how old he was. Not that forty-eight was exactly ancient, but at times he felt no more than half that.

Kevin glanced at the bed, considered spending more time making it up, then admitted the one or two minutes it cost him wouldn't be enough to make much difference. He might as well get into the kitchen and face the music.

It was going to be even worse than he'd thought, he decided as he saw Lacey's exhausted expression. She was clinging to that cup of tea as if it were her only lifeline. Her streaked blond hair tumbled loose across her shoulders, inviting his touch, but the look in her eyes when she saw him was forbidding.

"Good morning," he said cautiously, noting that she'd chosen a bright yellow blouse as if to defy her mood.

"Good morning. Would you like breakfast? I could fix you something."

"Tea and toast will do. I'll fix it."

As he popped the bread into the toaster, poured the tea, then brought everything to the table, he stole surreptitious glances at her. She was as still as could be, but there was nothing calm about her. He sensed that turbulent emotions were seething just below the surface. Her gaze was mostly directed down at the tea, but he could see the sorrow and wariness whenever she dared to glance his way.

"Kevin."

"Lacey."

The blurted words were practically simultaneous. With his glance he indicated deference.

Given her chance she looked uncertain. "We can't go on like this. I thought we could, but I was wrong."

"I know," he agreed.

She looked at him then, straight into his eyes, and to his amazement she looked a little helpless and more than a little vulnerable.

"I don't know where to begin," she said finally.

"At the beginning," he suggested, too glibly, judging from the look she shot him.

"That was too long ago to count," she said, but her tone was just a bit lighter. "Can you remember what it was like when we first got married?"

"Yes. At least I think I can. Why don't you tell me what you remember."

"I remember getting up in the morning filled with excitement and anticipation. I remember rushing through the day, reminding myself of every detail so I could share it with you that night. I remember how we talked about everything, every nuance of our lives, every decision, every hope, every dream." She sighed wistfully. "I thought that was the way it would always be."

"I suppose I did, too," he admitted. "It wasn't very realistic of either of us."

"Maybe not."

"Is that all you want back, Lacey? Just the sharing?"

"No, of course not." Her gaze met his, then slipped away. "We had the same vision, then. Somewhere along the way that's what we lost."

"Did we?" he argued. "Don't we both still want the world to be a better place? Don't we both care about family more than anything?"

"I thought we did."

"But?"

"We have such different ways of acting on it. You see a charity, and you need to write a check. You want a home, so you hire people to run it. You believe in family, but not in spending the time it takes to nurture one."

"So I'm still the one at fault," he said, unable to keep the impatience out of his voice. "Only me."

"Of course not," she said at once. "The difference between us is that I've tried every way I could think of to tell you what I need, but you've never once given me a clue about what you want from me anymore. Whatever the housekeeper fixes for dinner is fine. Whatever I wear is fine. However I spend my days is fine." Her tone mimicked him. Her chin rose another notch. "Even the sex began to seem more like habit than the spontaneous passion we used to have."

Kevin stared at her in astonishment. "That's ridiculous," he said defensively.

"Is it? Is it really?" She drew in a deep breath, then braced her hands against the table, almost as if she needed support for whatever she had to say. "Were you having an affair, Kevin?" she asked point blank. "That would explain so much."

Kevin felt as if she'd punched him in his midsection. Shocked, he simply stared at her. He couldn't imagine an accusation that would have thrown him more.

"Well?" she demanded defiantly.

"An affair? Where on earth would you get a ridiculous idea like that?"

"Come on, Kevin. Don't act too stunned. You wouldn't be the first man to have an affair. I can't even count the number of husbands we know who openly play around on their wives.''

"Not me, dammit. Not me."

When she continued to look skeptical, he said, "Lacey, I can honestly say that I never even contemplated breaking our marriage vows, much less acted on the thought."

"Is that the truth, Kevin?" she asked softly, her gaze searching his.

He realized then that perhaps more than all the other complaints, all the other differences, this was the one at the root of all their troubles. She couldn't even bring herself to trust him anymore, not even on something as sacred as their marriage vows.

He could read the vulnerability in her eyes, the fear that he'd turned elsewhere for satisfaction, and the expression in her eyes made him ache.

"Darling, I love you. Only you. No matter what else has happened, that has never, ever changed. I've never wanted anyone the way I wanted you."

"Past tense," she observed ruefully.

"No," he swore, leaving his chair to gather her into his arms. She held herself so stiffly, refusing to yield to a comfort too easily offered.

"Present tense," he told her. "I want you now every bit as much as I did when we were a couple of kids discovering our hormones for the first time. Couldn't you tell that last night on the beach, or the night before that and the night before that?''

Apparently he had found the right words—or the right combination of words and touch, after all. He could see the relief slowly washing through her. The words, though, would never be enough. He had to show her how much he needed her, how beautiful he still found her.

''Come with me,'' he coaxed, brushing her hair back from her face. All thoughts of other issues, other problems faded in his need to convince her of this much at least. ''Let me put this crazy notion of yours to rest forever.''

Lacey was slow to accept, and he thought for a moment that she might not, using who-knew-what this time as an excuse. In that brief instant of hesitation, he weighed the future without her against the past and realized that nothing would ever be the same if he lost her.

Kevin slid his fingers through her hair until the silky curls tumbled free. The pad of his thumb traced her mouth, the full bottom lip that trembled beneath his touch.

''Please,'' he whispered, unable to hide the faint note of desperation. ''I need you, Lacey. I need you now.''

Her fingers came up and linked with his, and the shadows slid away from her eyes, revealing the sheen of tears. "I need you, too," she said.

He would have swept her into his arms in a romantic gesture if he hadn't caught the forbidding look on her face when she realized his intentions. He grinned ruefully. "It's only a few feet," he reminded her.

"Then surely my knees aren't so weak with longing that I can't walk there on my own," she said, surprising him with the dry humor.

His low chuckle slipped out and then they were both laughing. He slanted a kiss across her mouth, capturing the much too infrequent musical sound of her laughter and the taste of milky tea.

"You could always make me laugh," he said.

"I know," she said with a devilish twinkle in her eyes.

But then her hands were at work on the snap of his jeans and he no longer felt the least bit like laughing. He sucked in his breath when her fingers skimmed across denim seeking the already hard shaft beneath.

"Wait," Kevin said urgently, pulling her down to the bed with him and pinning her hands away from him. He touched his mouth to hers, savoring again the taste, the texture, the heat. Her lips, her tongue had always fascinated him. He could have spent hours absorbed in no more than the nuances of her kisses. But all the while, he worked to rid her of her blouse, her bra, her jeans and panties, just so he could skim fingertips over velvet flesh and tight golden curls.

Soft whispers turned to anxious moans as he came closer and closer to the moist warmth at the apex of her thighs. She struggled to free her hands and when he released her at long last, she used her hands to torment him, to stroke and caress, to soothe and inflame. She slid her hands under his sweater, tangling her fingers in the hairs on his chest, seeking masculine nipples, her gaze locked with his.

She shifted then, and he couldn't take his eyes off the pale softness of her hands as they curved around him, stroking until he thought he would explode from the intensity.

Each of them battled to give, to shower the other with all the love, all the satisfaction that had been withheld for so long. And when the giving pulled them higher and higher, they had to release that last thread of control and learn to accept the unselfish offering.

Lacey came apart first, her body arching, her skin slick with sweat, her eyes filled with so much joy that Kevin was drawn along with her.

When both of them had caught their breath, when the caresses had slowed, he looked into her eyes and promised more. This time, joined together, they traveled even farther, soared even higher.

He couldn't recall a time when they had asked more of each other or given so much. It was proof, beyond all doubt, that what they had was strong enough to last a lifetime.

They slept then, close together, their breath mingling as morning turned to afternoon.

It was only later, in the aftermath of that extraordinary lovemaking, that Kevin said, "This was never, ever the problem between us, Lace."

He swept his hand over the curve of her hip, lingered on the fullness of her breast to prove his point. He knew at once when her body tensed, knew instinctively that his meaning had registered in a way that went beyond the reassuring simplicity of the words. He had unwittingly opened a new door, rather than closing an old one.

"Then what was it?" she demanded softly. "You can't deny that for a time we never touched, not in any way that mattered. Were you just too busy? Too tired? What?"

Kevin tried to find the answers she needed to hear. He searched his heart for things he had never before been willing to put into words. Maybe even thoughts he'd never dared to acknowledge, even to himself.

"Too distracted is probably closer to the truth. I lost sight of what was important," he admitted slowly, as he carefully sorted through explanations.

"After all those years of rebelling, of making my own way, I got caught up in my father's dreams after all. Halloran Industries became important to me. I wanted to make it work. I wanted to have a legacy for our son.''

Lacey sat up then, dragging the sheet around her and knotting it above her breasts. Sitting cross-legged before him, she watched him closely in the way that she had of trying to read his innermost, unspoken thoughts. Apparently she came up wanting, because she shook her head.

''But that doesn't explain it. Why should that have driven a wedge between us? I always wanted whatever it took to make you happy.''

''You did,'' he agreed, ''or at least you gave it lip service whenever I tried to discuss my decision about Halloran Industries with you.''

''Lip service?'' she repeated, obviously stung by the charge.

''Yes. As long as what I wanted didn't change too substantially, you went along with it. But along the way I did change substantially. Not necessarily for the best. My needs changed and, no matter what you said aloud, I could see the way you really felt about those changes. It was as if I'd betrayed you, as if I'd betrayed what we'd once fought so hard against. You kept your ideals. I caved in. The accusation was there every time I looked into your eyes.''

As the full meaning of Kevin's words sank in, Lacey was shocked by his interpretation of what had gone on between them. "Did I ever say that?"

"You didn't have to. Like I said, it was in your eyes every time you looked at me. When I went to work for Dad, when I bought the house, I always sensed you were making a judgment and that I was coming up short."

"That was your own guilt talking, not me."

"Then why did you begin to withdraw?"

Withdraw? Her? How could that have been, she wondered. "I never meant to do that," she said with total honesty. "Kevin, I didn't hate your job or that house because they represented some evil standard of living. I worried because it seemed to me that you took the job for all the wrong reasons, that you took it because you thought it was your obligation to your father and to Jason and me."

"And the house? What about that?"

"I hated the house because it no longer seemed like our home, not the way our first house did. I couldn't keep the new one up, so we hired a maid and a housekeeper and a gardener. All the things I loved to do, all the things that I needed to do to take care of my family, to feel I was making a contribution were in the hands of strangers. I felt as if I'd been cast adrift."

Her claim hovered in the air until at last he said softly, wearily, "I never knew that."

"Because we never talked about it. That was my fault, I suppose. I should have explained how I felt."

Kevin caressed her cheek, the touch light and fleeting. "I just wanted you to have everything," he explained. "It never occurred to me that in giving you all that, I was taking away something that you felt was more precious."

"My identity," she said quietly. "How could you not have known, Kevin, that all I ever wanted was you?"

Something in Kevin's face shut down at her words. Lacey had meant them to be reassuring, but it was clear he hadn't taken them that way.

"What's wrong?" she asked, as an odd chill seemed to invade her.

For the longest time he didn't answer, and during that time she was sure she could hear every tick of the clock on the bedstand, feel every anxious beat of her heart.

Finally, his eyes troubled, he met her gaze. There was so much raw anguish in his face that she was trembling even before he spoke.

"I can't be your whole world, Lace. I just can't."

"But that's not what I meant," she protested.

He shook his head. "Isn't it? The pressure of that, it's more than I can handle."

Stunned by the bleak finality of his tone, she could only watch as he left the bed, grabbed his clothes and went into the bathroom. She was still helplessly staring after him when he left the house just moments later.

Chapter Fourteen

No one was more stunned than Kevin at the words that had popped out of his mouth just before he'd left the house. Where had those thoughts come from? How had he gone for so many years without the vaguest sense that there was so much resentment buried deep inside him? A shrink would surely have a field day with that one.

As he walked on the beach, oblivious to the sun's heat and the pounding of the waves, Kevin tried hard not to remember the quick flash of hurt and confusion in Lacey's eyes. His implied accusation that her dependence on him had somehow weighed him down had been cruel, especially since he couldn't even explain what was behind it.

Hell, he was the one who'd carved out his role as her protector early on. He'd liked feeling ten feet tall when she looked to him for answers to everything from math lessons to politics. If some of that uneven balance had carried over into their marriage, wasn't that as much his fault as hers?

What worried him more than casting blame for that was the discovery that he had hidden such feelings from himself. Were they really buried in his subconscious or had they merely been a quick, defensive reaction to the guilt he'd accepted too readily for far too long?

Lacey was perfect. Their marriage was perfect. Wasn't that why he'd wanted so desperately to win her back? Surely he wasn't one of those men who clung to the past, simply because they couldn't bear the thought of change.

But if that were so, if he were convinced that everything was so perfect, why did he have this nagging sense that he'd been fooling himself? Had he simply grown comfortable in the role of martyr, accepting the blame heaped on him and feeling noble for ignoring his own doubts?

No, dammit! He did love Lacey. He tried that claim out in his head. It rang just as true as it ever had. Okay, then, he wasn't stark raving mad. He was just mixed up, confused, maybe a little exhausted from all the tension. He wasn't thinking clearly.

Hard as he tried, though, he couldn't easily dismiss what had happened. Those words had come from somewhere and he'd darned well better figure out where before he went back to face Lacey again. If their marriage hadn't always been so perfect, after all, he'd better be able to explain what had been lacking from his point of view. She knew what she thought of as his failings as clearly as if she'd carried an itemized list of his sins around in her head.

But no matter how desperately Kevin tried to find a precise, clear-cut answer, he couldn't. So, he thought with a sigh filled with regrets, it wasn't going to be so easy for them, after all. They were going to have to struggle for answers.

He supposed they were among the lucky ones. They still had the will to fight for their marriage. They had their love. They had this new-found honesty, as painful as it was. He hadn't a doubt in his head that they would make it, as long as they didn't shy away from the truth.

He walked until the sky dimmed and the wind picked up. The biting chill cut through his jacket, but worse was the chill he felt deep inside.

For years now he had not taken the time to be terribly introspective, but suddenly he had the sense that something very precious was on the line. He had to figure out exactly why there had been that vague anger behind his words, that hint of something too long repressed. Theories weren't the answer. He needed facts. He needed to pinpoint the cause, narrow it down to a specific moment or an evolution. He had to understand what was in his heart as clearly as what was in his head.

Kevin thought back to the early days of his marriage, days crammed with too much to do and so much tenderness and love. He and Lacey had both worked like demons at demanding, and often thankless, jobs. Then they had spent long hours side by side volunteering for causes they both believed in. Each night they had tumbled into bed, exhausted, but filled with exhilaration.

That period of their lives had been incredibly special. There was absolutely no doubt in his mind about that. Thinking about those days brought smiles, even laughter. Never pain.

But that time had been far too short, now that he thought about it. When Jason was born barely a year after the wedding, things began to change. Lacey took her maternity leave and seemed to blossom before his eyes as she took care of their son. She turned their cramped apartment into a real home, and there were tempting, creative dinners on the table.

Soon any thoughts of her returning to work, any time for volunteering vanished in a sea of household demands. They moved into the house Jason now owned. Nothing ever quite went back to the way it had been.

And he'd resented it, he realized with a sense of shock that actually brought him to a standstill. All these years he had resented the way things had changed, and yet he'd never said a word, hadn't even identified the cause of his mild dissatisfaction.

If he had changed as she had accused him of so often, then so had she. They had never once dealt with that.

He thought he understood why. Unlike Lacey, he had kept the resentment so deeply buried that only now could he recognize the subtle way it had affected everything between them.

If Lacey was going to conform to a more traditional pattern, if she was going to content herself with a home and motherhood, then why shouldn't he do the male equivalent of caving in? At least that must have been the subliminal message at work on him when he'd finally made the decision to go to work at Halloran Industries. How many decisions after that had been affected in the same way?

To top it off, he'd then had to deal with Lacey's unspoken disapproval, along with his own burden of guilt about becoming more and more like his father with each day that passed. He'd called it growing up, but obviously deep inside he'd never truly believed it.

Explaining all of this to her after all this time wasn't going to be easy. He needed some time to sort through it all himself, time to be sure that the answers he'd come up with were valid. Time, in fact, to discover if his marriage was something he really wanted to succeed.

The last seemed like blasphemy. Of course he wanted it to succeed. That was the one given in all this, the one thing he'd never questioned.

Until now, he reminded himself. Lord knows, he had questions now. Unfortunately he didn't have the luxury of time to find the answers, time to examine and come to terms with these raw new discoveries about himself. Lacey was waiting for him.

Kevin's pace picked up, almost in spite of all the doubts tumbling through his poor, pitiful, aching head. That alone should have told him something. He needed to get back to her, to share his thoughts and hear her reaction to them. Lacey had always had a knack for cutting through his self-delusion.

Until now, he reminded himself ruefully. Now when it probably meant more than anything.

When he got back to the house, he found her sitting in the living room, almost lost in the shadowy darkness. He flipped on a light and felt his heart wrench at the tears tracking down her cheeks. He wanted to go to her. He wanted to hold her, comfort her.

Instinctively he started toward her, then stopped himself. They needed to air these raw emotions, not soothe them away with meaningless promises.

"Are you okay?" he asked.

"Sure. Terrific," she said with a defiant lift of her chin. She couldn't hide the way it trembled, though. It reminded him of their first meeting so long ago, and his heart ached for her.

And for himself.

"I think maybe this had been the most difficult couple of hours in my entire life," he said finally, sinking into a chair across from her and dragging a hand through his hair.

Eyes shimmering with tears clashed with his. "It hasn't been much of a picnic for me, either."

"No, I'm sure it hasn't been. I'm sorry."

She shrugged. "For what? For being honest? I asked for it, didn't I?"

"But I think we both thought it was going to be a simple matter of airing a few gripes, vowing to try harder and then forgetting all about it."

"Yeah," she said, "silly us."

"There is a bright side," he told her, trying to earn a smile.

"Oh?"

"We haven't had to pay a fortune for shrinks to get to this point."

"Now that is something to stand up and cheer about," she said, her voice steadier at last.

Tears still clung to the ends of her lashes, but she looked stronger somehow, as if she could withstand anything. Perhaps he'd underestimated her ability to stand on her own and overestimated the depth of her need for him.

Whichever it was, Kevin knew in that instant that he had never loved Lacey more. Whatever faint, lingering doubts he had had about that had fled. His heart still turned over at the sight of her. His head still demanded that he protect her from the sort of hurt he himself had inflicted on her. Old habits obviously died hard.

"Feel like talking?" he asked. "Or should we take some time out? Go to a movie or something?"

She met his gaze evenly. "Hey, it couldn't get much worse than this. Let's get it all out now. I don't think I could concentrate on a movie, anyway."

Her glib words were sheer bravado, but Kevin knew there would never be a better time, that what he had to say would hurt whenever he said it. It was better to get everything out in the open now, so they could begin to pick up the pieces.

If there were any left to pick up. Dear God, why did that thought creep in so often? It terrified him. Like an earthquake, it seemed to shake the very foundation of his life.

He stared at the fire before he spoke, gathering courage, censoring harsh accusations. "It's funny," he began slowly. "I never knew that I felt quite so angry until the words came out of my mouth earlier."

Lacey regarded him intently, as if she were weighing his words. "I still don't understand," she said finally. "You talk about feeling pressured. Why? What did I ever do to make you feel that way? I built my life around making you happy."

"Exactly. Instead of caring about the world as you always had, you limited your concerns to just me and our family. I guess I felt that you had betrayed me long before it was the other way around."

"Betrayed you how?" she asked, looking wounded. "By loving you? By needing you?"

"By changing," he said simply.

"But I'm not the one who changed," she protested.

"Yes. Maybe you can't see it, but I can. You were always strong and independent. You always had this clear vision of what you wanted out of life, what we should be doing to make the world a better place to live. There we were, these two intrepid souls going off to tilt at windmills. We were so self-righteous, I suppose, thinking that we knew more than our parents, that we could fix all their mistakes."

"We did fix some things," she reminded him, a little sadly it seemed.

"Maybe some," he agreed. "Then we had Jason and everything changed. The entire focus of your world centered on our son and on me."

"We had a new baby, Kevin. What did you expect?"

"I'm not talking about the first month or even the first year. I could have understood that. But that absorption with our own narrow world didn't end. I began to feel pressured for the first time since I had known you. No man should ever have to carry the burden of being totally responsible for another person's happiness."

With a growing sense of shock and dismay, Lacey listened to Kevin's version of what had happened to their marriage and tried to reconcile it with her own. It wasn't that she could not accept part of the blame. It was simply that the way he described the changes in their relationship weren't the way she remembered things at all.

There had been so much magic once. There had been so many times over the past couple of weeks that she had thought for sure they were recapturing it. Now she knew that had been only a naive dream.

This time, magic wasn't quite enough. Lacey struggled with the fact that the life she'd chosen for herself—the role of homemaker in which she'd been so happy, could never be quite the same again. Jason was married now and her husband didn't need her to see to his every need, in fact resented her devotion.

Could it possibly be true that the very things she accused him of were true of her, as well? Was she no longer the generous person who thought only of helping others? Had she lost the vision they'd once shared, just as she believed he had? It had been only recently that she'd rediscovered a sense of activism in the form of the housing project in which Paula had involved her.

"Maybe I should leave, go back to Boston," she said finally, expressing a thought that had already come to her while Kevin had been gone. In fact, her mind was already made up despite the tentative way she'd phrased it.

Kevin regarded her angrily, as if the suggestion were yet another betrayal. "Leave? Now? Lacey, we're just starting to get somewhere. You can't run away now."

"It's not running. I just need to find some answers to questions I didn't even realize existed. What you've said makes a lot of sense. I was so busy bemoaning the fact that you were no longer the man I married that I never saw that I was no longer the woman you'd married. I need to go find Lacey Grainger again.''

"Lacey Halloran," he corrected sharply. "I never meant for you to leave."

Lacey moved to his side, hunkered down and placed her hand over his. She caressed his knuckles, wishing she weren't responsible for the fact that he'd clenched his hands into tight, angry fists.

"I know leaving wasn't your idea. But I have a lot of thinking to do."

"And you can't do it here?"

"No," she said sadly. "When I'm with you, it's all I want and that's wrong. You've said so yourself."

Kevin sighed deeply, then looked resigned. "When will you go?"

"If it's okay with you, I'll wait until morning."

"Sure."

"Will you go back into town with me or do you want to stay out here?"

"I think I'll wait here. If I go back, I won't do the thinking I need to do, either. I'll end up going back to the office."

She nodded and stood up. "I'll go pack."

She was almost out the door when he said, "Lacey?"

"Yes?" she said without turning around.

"The one thing I know without question is that I do love you. I'll be here waiting for you when you're ready to talk again."

She felt the salty sting of tears. Her lower lip trembled. "I love you, too," she said in a voice that quavered slightly.

She couldn't quite bring herself to promise that she would be back. She had no idea where the coming days of self-discovery were likely to lead her.

Chapter Fifteen

Naturally the most depressing day of Kevin's life had dawned sunny and mild. The beauty of the sunrise, the gentleness of the morning breeze seemed to mock him. A day like this should have been gray and gloomy, with the threat of a blizzard maybe. Barring that, a good, steady rain would have done.

Instead, he had to contend with clear skies and a temperature that beckoned. He'd tried his best to make it work to his advantage, but the time was fast approaching when Lacey would be pulling out of the driveway and heading back to Boston.

Saying goodbye to his wife—and quite possibly to his marriage—was one of the most difficult things

Kevin ever had to do. It would be a thousand times harder this time than it had been months ago when Lacey had first made the decision to move to a place of her own. Or maybe he'd just forgotten the pain of that goodbye.

Already he had delayed her departure by several hours. He had talked her into one last walk on the beach in the glorious morning sunlight. Then he had convinced her that she had to eat before facing such a long drive. He'd insisted on a picnic on the beach. Then he'd asked her to pick up a few last-minute things in town so he wouldn't have to call on the neighbors. She had seized each excuse far more readily than a woman who was anxious to go.

Finally, though, he had run out of excuses. The only one left to him was a plea for her to reconsider leaving at all, and that one he had promised himself not to use. Though yesterday he had fought her going, he knew that she was right. They needed time apart to sort through everything, to figure out exactly who they were.

"You'll call when you get to town?" he asked as he carefully closed the car door.

"I'll call."

She glanced up at him, her blue eyes shimmering with unshed tears. She blinked hurriedly, then looked away. He could barely hear her when she asked, "You'll be careful? You'll take care of yourself?"

"Of course," he promised. "You don't think I'm going to undo all the good you've done with those nourishing soups, do you?"

"Are you sure you don't want me to take you to rent a car?"

"No. You'll be back before I need one," he said, though there was a forced sound to his optimism. He touched a finger to her chin and tilted her head up until he could gaze directly into her eyes. "I'll miss you."

"Me, too." She hesitated, then reached for the key and started the engine. "I should get started."

"Right. Drive carefully." He stepped back from the car.

"I always do."

He couldn't think of one more thing to say to make her linger. He reminded himself again that her decision to leave was the right one, the only one.

So why did he feel a lump the size of Texas lodged in his throat as he watched her go? Why did he feel this aching sense of abandonment, of loneliness and loss, when the car wasn't even out of sight?

Lacey prayed that she would be able to go back to Boston without anyone knowing. She didn't want Jason and Dana hovering. She certainly didn't want Brandon charging in to save the day. Why hadn't she extracted a promise from Kevin not to tell them?

Hopefully he would have his own reasons for keeping quiet.

She turned the car radio on full blast, to an oldies station, hoping to drown out her thoughts. Instead, every song dragged her back down memory lane. She cried all the way home—big, sloppy tears that left her blouse soaking wet and her eyes red.

It was dark when she finally got back into town. She had never felt lonelier than she did when she turned the key in the lock of the apartment she had rented months earlier. She went through the living room, bedroom and kitchen switching on lights. She flipped on the stereo because the silence seemed oppressive. This time, at least, she was wise enough to avoid old favorites.

The apartment wasn't so bad, though after the home she and Kevin had shared, it seemed little bigger than one of their walk-in closets. The furniture was slightly shabby, but comfortable. She reminded herself that in many ways she had been happy during her months here. There had been a contentment, though she'd always felt that something was missing. Not something material, just Kevin.

Just Kevin, she thought mockingly, as if he were no more important than a comfortable bed or a faded print of some masterpiece. The truth of the matter, though, was that she could have been happy here for the rest of her days, if Kevin had been here to share it.

She supposed that was just one example of that dependence he'd complained about.

Enough, she decided. Tomorrow would be soon enough to tackle the future. She concentrated instead on settling in. It took her no time at all to put her clothes away, to shove her suitcases into the back of the cramped closet. Making herself a pot of tea wasted ten minutes at best.

And then she had to face the fact that she was really and truly alone. Always before she had known in the back of her mind that leaving here and going home was her decision, that Kevin would welcome her back. It was entirely possible after the talk they had had last night that he would have second thoughts about resuming their marriage.

She was startled when the phone rang. She considered not answering it, then worried that it might be Kevin. He'd looked fine when she'd driven off, but something could have happened since then. And he was the only one who knew she'd left the Cape, the only one who would expect to find her here.

"Hello," she said hesitantly.

"Lacey, it's me."

"Kevin. Are you okay?"

"Fine. More to the point, how are you? You promised to call."

"I'm fine," she said, clutching the phone tightly. So, she thought, they were reduced to polite chit-chat.

"I'm sorry. I just got in a half hour ago. I was getting settled."

"Everything's okay, then? You've locked the door? Checked the windows?"

A smile crept up on her. "Yes. Kevin, this apartment is perfectly safe."

"Lacey, the security system consists of an old man who'd sell out his own mother for a bottle of booze."

"That's not true. Charley is very careful about who he lets in. Besides, he's not on at night."

As soon as the words were out of her mouth, she realized they'd been a mistake.

"What do you mean he's not on at night?" Kevin demanded. "Who is?"

"Actually, there's a buzzer system."

"My God."

"Kevin, it's fine."

"Sure, okay. I guess you know what you're doing," he said wearily.

"Thanks for checking on me, though," she said, reluctant now to cut the connection. Kevin's concern, even under these tense circumstances, made her feel warm and cherished.

But of course that was what this was all about—proving whether she could stand on her own two feet without him there to protect her. She wasn't sure which of them needed to know the answer to that the most.

* * *

Lacey spent the next day restocking her refrigerator, going through the mail and cleaning the apartment. It gave her one whole day of reprieve from thinking about the agonizing decision she had to make.

By afternoon, a late spring cold front was pushing through, bringing rain and icy winds. The skies turned dark and miserable by five o'clock, mirroring her mood.

By eight she was ready to scream. Fearful of what too much introspection might reveal, she picked up the phone and called Paula Gethers. She sensed that staying busy, that finding a new purpose to her life was going to be the most critical thing to come of the next days or weeks.

"How's the house coming?" Lacey asked without preamble, hoping to get her friend off on her favorite topic before she could pick up on any unwitting signals Lacey might be sending out.

"Okay," Paula said, then promptly added, "Lacey, what's wrong?"

So much for fooling an old friend. "Who says anything is wrong?" she said anyway.

"I do, and I'm never wrong about these things."

"Look, I was just wondering if you could use my help tomorrow. That's all."

"I can always use your help, but something tells me you want to hit nails so you won't break up the furniture."

"If you're suggesting I sound depressed, you're right."

"Actually, I would have said angry."

"Maybe that, too. But I don't want to talk about it," she said firmly. "Not now and definitely not tomorrow."

"Then I will see you first thing in the morning and I will keep my opinion of your sorry state of mind to myself."

Lacey sighed. "Thanks on all counts."

"Hon, you don't have to thank me for letting you work your buns off. As for the rest, you may not want to thank me after you've had time to think about it. You sound like you could use someone to talk to. Just remember, I'm here if you change your mind."

Paula said goodbye and hung up before Lacey could reply that the last thing she needed right now was more talk. She and Kevin had done enough of that to last a lifetime. Maybe if they hadn't spent so darn much time digging below the surface of their problems, she wouldn't be questioning the very foundation of her life right now.

She had built her life on loving and being loved by Kevin. Without him, what was left? Her relationship with her son and daughter-in-law to be sure, but they certainly didn't need her hanging around twenty-four hours a day.

Her thoughts were starting to be so depressing that she made the mistake of grabbing the phone without thought when it rang again. Any interruption would be better than more of these dark reminders of the state of her marriage.

The sound of Brandon's voice snapped her back to the present. Any interruption except this one, she corrected, wondering if she dared to hang up in his ear.

"Good. You're there. I'm coming over," he announced.

"Brandon, don't," she pleaded, then realized that she was talking to herself. Her father-in-law had already hung up.

If she hadn't been so furious, she might have laughed. Brandon was reacting totally in character. He was as predictable when it came to loving his family as, well, as she was. The comparison was the most amusing thing of all.

Lacey briefly considered fleeing, but figured a stint in the French Foreign Legion wouldn't take her far enough. She satisfied her need for some illusion of control by letting him lean on the buzzer downstairs for five full minutes before letting him in.

Brandon glared at her when she finally opened the door, then breezed straight past her, carelessly tossing his Halloran cashmere coat over the back of a chair.

He left his umbrella dripping all over the kitchen floor, then stalked into the living room. It looked smaller than ever with him prowling from one end to the other, a disapproving scowl on his face. He rubbed his fingers over the cheap upholstery on the sofa and shook his head, his dismay unmistakable.

"I'm delighted to see you, too," she said dryly, when it looked as if it might be a long time before he got down to saying exactly what was on his mind.

"What's the point of making small talk? We both know why I'm here."

"I doubt that," Lacey retorted.

He shot her a puzzled glance as her implication sank in. "What the devil's that supposed to mean?"

"It means that you couldn't begin to know what's gone on between Kevin and me the last couple of days, not unless your son has broken a lifelong cardinal rule and confided in you."

"I know you're here and he's still on Cape Cod."

"And how did you discover that?"

"I drove out there today."

Lacey's eyebrows rose at that.

"I had some papers to drop off," he retorted without a trace of defensiveness. "Kevin tried to cover for your absence, but he's a lousy liar. That's enough to tell me you two fools still haven't settled your differences."

"Brandon, you can't charm me into doing what you want," Lacey said dryly.

He gave her a sharp glance. "I wasn't trying to charm you. Dammit all, can't you stop jumping down my throat for five minutes and listen to what I have to say?"

Lacey drew in a deep breath and apologized. "You're right," she said, sitting down opposite him. "Would you like something? A cup of tea, maybe?"

"I came here for a real heart-to-heart, not to see if you're up on your social graces."

"Fine. Say whatever you want to say."

He nodded in satisfaction. "Years ago I did you a grave disservice. Nobody's sorrier for that than I am. You and Kevin came pretty close to lighting up a room with the kind of love you had. When the two of you stood up to me, I thought there'd never come a day when something more powerful than me would come along and change that."

She found herself grinning at the high esteem in which he held his own power.

"What's so danged funny?" he grumbled.

"Nothing," she said. "Go on."

"I'm not here to ask you again what your differences are. Kevin's old enough to plead his own case."

To her astonishment, he actually looked uneasy. Before she could figure out what to make of that, he said, "I just want you to know if this has anything at all to do with those old days, I'm sorry for what happened and nothing would make me happier than to see the two of you back together.''

Touched by the apology, even though it had come nearly three decades too late, Lacey found herself reaching for his hand and clasping it. "Brandon, this isn't about you. I swear it.''

"Halloran Industries then? You never did want Kevin to work there.''

"That's not true. I just wanted him to make his own choice, not to be bulldozed by you.''

"Well, if it's not me and it's not my company, what is it?'' he demanded as if the thought of anything else were totally preposterous.

Lacey burst out laughing at that. "And Kevin complained because *I* had a narrow world.''

Brandon glowered at her. "What's that supposed to mean?''

"It means, you crotchety old man, that I adore the single-minded purpose with which you protect what's yours. Kevin obviously inherited that from you.''

Brandon was shaking his head. "You think he's anything like me?''

"A lot more than either of you suspect, I think. Thank you for coming by. It means a lot.''

"You going back there in the morning?''

"No,'' she said firmly.

Brandon looked disappointed. "My powers of per-
suasion must be off a little."

"Don't worry. I'm just a tougher sell than your run-
of-the-mill client."

"What are you going to do?"

"Tomorrow I'm going to build a house."

He regarded her as if she'd suddenly started speaking in Swahili. "Am I supposed to understand what
that means?"

"No," she said, laughing.

"Good. I'd hate to think I'd started losing my wits,
when I have some plans for the future I've been
thinking about. If I could just get the two of you settled and get that great grandbaby born, I might start
thinking about my own life."

This time it was Lacey's turn to be confused. "Am
I supposed to know what you're talking about?"

He gave her a wink. "Nope. This business of keeping secrets goes both ways."

Lacey felt her spirits begin to climb just a little as
she arrived at the housing site in the morning. The
thought of what the half-finished house before her
would mean to some family was gratifying. Maybe she
couldn't do much to fix her own life, but she could do
her part to help someone else get a new start.

She wandered around the house in search of Paula
or Dave, so she could get an assignment. She found

Paula atop a ladder. Her husband, his hair tied back in a ponytail, was holding the ladder steady with one hand. The other was sliding slowly up the back of Paula's denim-clad leg in an intimate caress.

Lacey felt the sting of tears as she listened to their familiar bickering. There wasn't a hostile note in the exchange, just the fond give and take of two people who'd found their own shorthand way of communicating.

When Dave's hand reached Paula's bottom, she turned and glared down at him. "You're not helping, David Gethers," she grumbled, but Lacey could clearly hear the amusement in her friend's voice.

"How can you say that?" he inquired innocently.

"Because I need to concentrate on what I'm doing here, instead of wondering where that roving hand of yours is heading."

"Don't you worry about that. You go right on doing whatever you need to do."

"If I have to come down off of this ladder," Paula warned with mock ferocity, "you are going to be one sorry man. Go check on the plumbers or something."

"It's the *or something* I'm interested in."

"Dave!"

"Okay, okay," he finally said with weary resignation. He turned and caught sight of Lacey.

"The woman is a trial," he grumbled. "Maybe you can explain to her that there are more important things than checking shingles or whatever she's doing up there.''

Lacey laughed. ''I doubt I'm the right person to be giving anyone advice on priorities.''

Paula peered down at her and immediately descended. ''Good. You're here.''

''Ready, willing and able,'' Lacey confirmed. ''What's my assignment?''

''First things first. Come with me,'' Paula steered her around the corner to an RV that served as a mobile office for the project. Inside, she held up a pot of coffee. ''Want some?''

Lacey hesitated, sensing that Paula had more on her mind than deciding whether to hand her a paintbrush or a screwdriver.

''Sure, why not?'' she said finally. She sat down on a corner of the office's one cluttered desk.

''So what did Kevin think when you told him about our project?'' Paula asked.

''He was very excited,'' Lacey said honestly. ''He wants to find a way to get Halloran Industries involved.''

''So why aren't you whooping for joy? Did you expect him to turn up here first thing this morning with a tool kit?''

Lacey sighed and set the cup of coffee aside. ''No, that's not it.''

''What then? Are you two reconciling or not?''

"I don't know."

Paula shook her head. "I don't get it. You love him. He loves you. What could be simpler than that?"

"He wants me to have my own interests."

"Like this project?"

Lacey shrugged. "I suppose."

"Come on, girl. Pick up the pace here. I'm getting lost. What do you want?"

"Let me see if I can figure out how to say this. The best thing about our relationship from the very beginning was that we always shared everything. Now he goes off to Halloran and I come here. I guess if anything, I'm envious of what you and Dave have. You share the same concerns. You work side by side."

"Can I assume that Kevin does not want to come over here and hammer things?"

"He wants to write checks."

"Hey, we need people like that, too. Don't even think about complaining about that."

Even as she and Paula talked, Lacey was struck by the first spark of an idea. Suddenly she felt her energy returning and her spirits mending. She grabbed Paula by the shoulders and hugged her.

"You are a genius," she declared. "I've got to run."

"Hey, I have you down for painting the entire living room today."

Lacey opened her purse and took out the hundred-dollar bill Kevin had given her as a joke a few nights earlier. "Pay someone," she said, handing it over. "I have a long drive ahead of me."

Chapter Sixteen

Lacey didn't waste a second before taking off for Cape Cod. Even though she was wearing paint-spattered jeans and an old blouse, she refused to go back to the apartment to change into something more presentable. What she had to say to Kevin was far more important than the way she looked. Half the time he didn't notice what she was wearing, anyway. She did pull off the bandana she'd tied around her head and ran her fingers through her hair to get rid of the tangles. At least there was no paint in it.

As she drove she considered all the implications of her idea. She couldn't figure out why she hadn't had this brainstorm before. During all those lonely months when she'd had nothing to do but think, no solution to the real problems in her marriage had come to her— probably because she hadn't even know exactly what those problems were. She'd focused too much on Kevin's health and not on the reasons he might have had for driving himself so hard.

Now, after less than forty-eight miserable hours apart, she had recognized the perfect answer, one that had been staring her in the face all along.

Perhaps the reason it seemed so easy now was because of the time she and Kevin had spent together on Cape Cod. In all of that painful self-analysis, they had brought themselves right to the brink of discovery. They might not have reconciled, but they had certainly laid all of the groundwork.

She had to be right about this, she thought as she reversed the drive she'd made only two days before. This time she felt so much more hopeful, not just about fulfilling her own needs, but about finding common ground that she and Kevin could share again, about recapturing that sense of purpose that had made their relationship so special.

Excitement and anticipation spilled through her. She deliberately turned on the oldies station and sang along with all the nostalgic hits, laughing at the happy memories that came back to crowd out the sad.

Her mood lasted until she turned into the driveway and saw Brandon's huge tank of a luxury car parked beside the house. Why was he back out here today? she wondered with a sinking feeling in the pit of her stomach. Why was he here when she so desperately needed to be alone with Kevin to see if they could finally fix their lives?

She drew in a deep breath and reminded herself that she was the one who'd said quite plainly that she wouldn't be coming back this morning. She had no one to blame but herself if her father-in-law had taken that to mean that it was up to him to keep Kevin company.

Of course, it was unlikely that Brandon was inside making soup or playing cards with Kevin. It was far more likely that he'd brought along a stack of work on the pretense of keeping his son occupied.

Feeling oddly uncertain, Lacey looked down at her old clothes and wondered if she ought to drive to the nearest boutique and buy something new. She could already envision Brandon's disapproval. Only her desire to share her idea before she had second thoughts prevented her from leaving. That and an awareness that it was long past time when she had to impress her father-in-law. His visit last night had finally put them on a friendlier footing that she was sure would last and grow.

She walked slowly up the walk, then found herself ringing the doorbell, rather than using her key. It was Kevin who opened the door.

His face looked haggard, as if he hadn't been getting nearly enough sleep since she'd left. There was a faint stubble on his cheeks that she yearned to reach out and caress. As tired as he looked, he'd never seemed more desirable. She wanted to throw herself into his arms and hold on until the dark days had gone for good.

And there was no mistaking the sudden spark of hope in his eyes when he saw her.

"You're back," he began inanely.

She understood the awkwardness, because she was feeling it as well, that and so much more. Trepidation, hope, love.

"Did you forget your key?"

She shook her head. "No. It's in my purse. I wasn't sure if I should use it."

"Lacey, this is your house as much as mine. More, probably."

She shrugged. "I realized that Brandon was here. I thought maybe, I don't know. I thought maybe I should wait and come back later when we could talk."

"Don't be ridiculous."

Just then Brandon appeared in the doorway to the living room. He searched her face, and then, as if he'd seen something he approved of—maybe her new-found confidence—he nodded. He turned at once and went back. It was more discretion than he'd ever displayed before.

"Come on in," Kevin said. "Dad and I were just finishing up."

"That's right," Brandon said, when they'd joined him. "I'll be on my way in just a minute."

It was clear though, that he had been ensconced in the living room for some time. Files were spread on the coffee table. As Lacey walked in, he punched a long series of numbers into a calculator. He nodded in satisfaction, jotted them down and then stood up.

"I'll leave you two. I'm sure you have a lot to discuss," he said, sounding as if he couldn't wait to get away. "Kevin, your instincts were exactly right. Those figures look good. I'll tell Jason to get on with things."

"That sounds good," Kevin said distractedly, his gaze still fixed on Lacey.

"You don't have to rush off," Lacey felt compelled to say to Brandon, though she wanted nothing more than to see him leave.

He grinned at her then. "You're a lousy liar, girl. Same as Kevin." He grabbed his coat and headed for the front door. "He's been trying to kick me out since I got here, but was too polite to come right out and say anything to my face."

"Drive carefully," she told him.

"Always do."

He left the room then, and Lacey stared out the front window while she waited for Kevin to come back. The last thing she overheard Brandon ask was when Kevin intended to get back to work.

"I'll have to let you know about that, Dad."

Lacey noticed Brandon had left the files and the calculator behind. She was tempted to toss the papers into the fireplace, but she left them on the coffee table, waiting to see what Kevin would do about them.

When he came back into the living room, his expression was cautious. "I'm surprised to see you back so soon," he began, his tone wary. He'd shoved his hands into the pockets of his jeans as if he couldn't quite figure out what else to do with them. He kept his distance, standing over by the fireplace, rather than joining her.

"No more surprised than I am to be back." She hesitated, then couldn't keep herself from asking, "You're not going to let Brandon push you into going back to work too soon, are you?"

He held up his hands. "Lacey, please don't start on that."

"I can't help it," she said, gesturing toward the mess on the coffee table. "Just look at what he's brought. There's enough there to keep you busy for a month."

"It's just Dad's way of making sure I'm not too lonely out here. He needed an excuse to come back."

Lacey wrestled with the idea of Brandon making up excuses for any of his actions. She couldn't imagine it.

Then again, in his relationship with his son, anything was possible. She suddenly realized that ever since Kevin had turned down that job at Halloran Industries years ago, Brandon quite probably had feared another rejection. He had never taken Kevin's presence at the company for granted.

At the same time, she and Kevin had taken each other for granted. They had operated for years now under the misguided notion that their relationship would always remain exactly the same. No wonder the past year had been so rocky.

"Are you ready to go back to work?" she asked finally.

"That depends."

"On?"

"What happens with us."

She shook her head. "No, you can't pin that decision on us, on me. What do you want to do with the rest of your life?"

She thought she knew the answer to that, but she had to hear him say it, had to know if the plan she'd devised made any sense at all.

"Actually, I do want to go back to Halloran," Kevin finally admitted with an obvious sigh of relief. "Tradition seems more important to me now. Working with my father and my son creates a bond that most men never have. I want that in my life. I didn't realize until recently how much I counted on that sense of continuity. I think I understand finally what it must have done to Dad when I walked away from it."

"Then you should go back."

He shook his head. "Not at the cost of destroying our marriage."

"Working at Halloran Industries could only destroy our marriage if we allow it to, if we attach some symbolic significance to it the way we did before," she said with a trace of impatience. "I think we're both past that. The important thing is to keep a balance in our lives, to keep the priorities straight. I don't want you obsessed with our marriage, any more than I want you obsessed with work. Isn't that what you were saying to me earlier?"

"Yes, but—"

"No," she said softly. "No *buts*, Kevin. This is about what you think is right for you."

"But I can't decide that in a vacuum. What do you need? What will make you happy?"

She turned to stare out the window as she searched for a way to explain what she was feeling, all the discoveries she'd made.

"I think maybe I actually have an answer to that," she said, finally turning back from the window and meeting his gaze. "I came back here so I could run it by you."

"So, tell me," he said.

Lacey drew in a deep breath. "I've been thinking, maybe we could form a Halloran Foundation, something we could work on together."

"Give away Halloran money?" Kevin teased, pretending to be scandalized by the very notion.

"Stop," she said. "I'm serious. You and your father have always been very generous, but this could be something we do in a more organized fashion."

Kevin's gaze was suddenly more intense. How many times had he looked just that way when they'd bounced ideas back and forth long ago? Her confidence had grown simply by seeing the way he respected what she thought.

"Go on," he said, the first hint of excitement in his voice. "I think I see where you're going with this."

Now, with that slim bit of encouragement, Lacey couldn't keep the enthusiasm out of her voice. "Okay. The way I see it, we'd set up a trust, an endowment, whatever. That would become the basis of the Foundation. That's where you and Brandon come in. You have to make the commitment to set aside the money to do this."

"And where do you fit in?"

"I thought I could evaluate applications, seek out the organizations and individuals that really need help, help establish programs. All those committees I've served on have taught me a lot about fund-raising and grant proposals and effectively run charities. I think I could weed out those that are poorly operated. I'd handle all the day-to-day things, the paperwork. The Halloran board would okay the grants."

Even as she talked, the tiny seed of an idea took root and flourished. She could see from the excitement in Kevin's eyes that he shared her enthusiasm.

"Yes," he said and added his ideas to hers until the Foundation seemed more a reality than a sudden inspiration that had come to her only hours ago.

"Don't you see, Kevin? The best part would be that we'd be doing it together, we'd share the same focus again, even if it's only one small aspect of what you do at Halloran."

He got up and moved to the window to stand behind her. His arms circled her waist. "I think it's the most wonderful, generous idea I've ever heard."

She turned in his arms until she could study him. She searched his face. "Really?"

"Really," he said, pressing a tender kiss to her forehead. Lacey felt her heart tumble.

"Do you think Brandon will go for it?" she asked, unable to keep the anxiety out of her voice.

"I think he'll love it."

"Kevin, I know this doesn't take care of everything. I know it's not some magical solution for us, but it's a start."

His lips touched hers then, capturing all the excitement and adding to it. Anticipation and joy touched off a spark that sent fire dancing through her veins.

"God, I love you," Kevin murmured, when he finally pulled away. "There are so many things I want to say to you, so many things we can do together, now that we know our marriage is here to stay. That is what you want, isn't it?"

"More than anything."

"What about the house?" he asked.

"Which house?" she asked, thoroughly puzzled by the change in direction.

"The one in Boston. Jason told me there's an interested buyer."

Lacey just stared at him. "You put it on the market?"

He nodded. "Before I left the hospital."

"Why?"

"It was awfully cold and lonely without you. Frankly, I kind of like it here. You and me, walking on the beach, warming up in front of a fire."

His hands swept over her, slowly stroking until she could imagine those nights of loving in front of the fire as vividly as he could. Then it didn't matter at all that she'd worn paint-spattered clothes, because he was sliding them off her, kissing every inch of her bare flesh until the fire in the hearth was nothing compared to the one deep inside her.

"Oh, my beautiful Lacey," he whispered, his gaze locked on hers. "I was so afraid you wouldn't come back, so afraid that my stupid pride would keep me from coming after you."

"Would you have come after me?" she asked, her voice breathless as he skimmed his fingers over her breasts.

"Yes. I realized finally that I have no pride at all where you're concerned. You hadn't been gone fifteen minutes when I knew that I was wrong to let you go. The only way to work things out was to do it together."

"Of course, I did do some pretty incredible thinking while I was away from you," she taunted.

"But look how much more clearly you're thinking now that we're back together."

She moaned as his fingers slid lower, over her belly and beyond to the precise spot where she yearned to be touched. She arched into the teasing touch. "This doesn't have anything to do with thinking," she told him when she could manage enough breath to say anything.

"That's not what I heard," he told her. "Making love starts in the head."

She slid her hand up his thigh until she reached the hard evidence of his arousal. "But that's not where it finishes, is it?" she taunted.

"Lacey, dearest, darling..."

"Yes?"

"If you keep that up—"

"That is my intention," she said.

"Lacey!"

"You had something else in mind?" she inquired pleasantly.

Kevin groaned. "No. No, I think you've got it."

"Then come here, please."

She arched her back as he drove into her. He pulled back, then entered her more slowly, establishing a tantalizing pace that was just one shade shy of unbearable.

"You're getting even, aren't you?" she asked him as he withdrew again.

"Would I do that?" he inquired, a glint of amusement in his eyes.

"You would." She concentrated very hard on not letting him drive her over the brink until she could take him with her.

Unfortunately she found it very difficult to concentrate on anything but the sensations that were throbbing through her with increasing intensity. The excitement she'd felt about the Halloran Foundation was nothing compared to the excitement generated by this one Halloran man.

"Kevin," she murmured finally.

"Yes."

"I think it's time to stop playing games."

The spark of amusement in his eyes gave way to a dark, burning desire as he lifted her hips and drove into her one last, exquisitely slow time. She felt herself tightening around him, holding him deep inside her until there was nothing left to say, nothing left to do except give herself over to the thrill of coming apart in his embrace.

For the longest time after their passion was spent, they stayed right where they were, curled up in front of the fire, the reflection of the flames dancing over their perspiration-slicked skin.

"So what do you think?" Kevin asked eventually.

"About what?"

"The house."

After the past half hour, there was only one possible answer as far as Lacey could tell. "Maybe we could make do with an apartment in the city and live on the Cape. I don't think I want to give up what we found out here."

"I certainly don't want to give up times like this," Kevin agreed.

"Are we really okay, though? I'm not dreaming the way I feel right now, am I?"

"Lacey, if it's a dream, then I'm caught up in the same one."

"But will it last?"

"Who can say? I can only promise you that from now on we'll never take each other for granted again.

Maybe what happened to us was all for the best. We both learned to appreciate what we have, and next time we'll both fight harder before we risk losing it.''

''Will there be a next time, then?'' she asked.

''I'm afraid so. There will always be crises in a marriage. Most people these days opt out at the first sign of trouble. I don't want us ever to do that again.''

''Is that your sense of Halloran honor talking?''

''No, Lacey, it's my love.''

* * * * *

Watch for Brandon's incredible story of
enduring love, Cherish, *coming next month*
from Silhouette Special Edition.

VOWS
A series celebrating marriage
by Sherryl Woods

To Love, Honor and Cherish—these were the words that three generations of Halloran men promised their women they'd live by. But these vows made in love are each challenged by the tests of time....

In October—Jason Halloran meets his match in *Love* #769;
In November—Kevin Halloran rediscovers love—with his wife—in *Honor* #775;
In December—Brandon Halloran rekindles an old flame in *Cherish* #781.

These three stirring tales are coming down the aisle toward you—only from Silhouette Special Edition!

Take 4 bestselling love stories FREE

Plus get a FREE surprise gift!

Silhouette
CHRISTMAS
Stories 1992

Experience the beauty of Yuletide romance with Silhouette
Christmas Stories 1992—a collection of heartwarming stories by
favorite Silhouette authors.

JONI'S MAGIC by Mary Lynn Baxter
HEARTS OF HOPE by Sondra Stanford
THE NIGHT SANTA CLAUS RETURNED by Marie Ferrarrella
BASKET OF LOVE by Jeanne Stephens

Also available this year are three popular early editions of
Silhouette Christmas Stories—1986, 1987 and 1988. Look for
these and you'll be well on your way to a complete collection
of the best in holiday romance.

Plus, as an added bonus, you can receive a FREE keepsake
Christmas ornament. Just collect four proofs of purchase from
any November or December 1992 Harlequin or Silhouette series
novels, or from any Harlequin or Silhouette Christmas
collection, and receive a beautiful dated brass Christmas
candle ornament.

Mail this certificate along with four (4) proof-of-purchase coupons, plus $1.50 postage and
handling (check or money order—do not send cash), payable to Silhouette Books, to: **In the
U.S.:** P.O. Box 9057, Buffalo, NY 14269-9057; **In Canada:** P.O. Box 622, Fort Erie, Ontario,
L2A 5X3.

ONE PROOF OF PURCHASE	Name: _____
	_____
	Address: _____
	_____
	City: _____
	State/Province: _____
SX92POP	Zip/Postal Code: _____

093 KAG